COLONEL SANDHURST TO
THE RESCUE

COLONEL SANDHURST TO THE RESCUE

Marion Chesney

Being the Fifth Volume of
The Poor Relation

Chivers Press   •   G.K. Hall & Co.
Bath, Avon, England   Thorndike, Maine USA

This Large Print edition is published by Chivers Press, England, and by G.K. Hall & Co., USA.

Published in 1995 in the U.K. by arrangement with the author.

Published in 1995 in the U.S. by arrangement with St. Martin's Press, Inc.

U.K. Hardcover ISBN 0–7451–2582–4 (Chivers Large Print)
U.K. Softcover   ISBN 0–7451–2583–2 (Camden Large Print)
U.S. Softcover   ISBN 0–8161–7415–6 (Nightingale Collection
                                       Edition)

The text of this Large Print edition is unabridged.
Other aspects of the book may vary from the original edition.

Set in 16 pt. New Times Roman.

Printed in Great Britain on acid-free paper.

British Library Cataloguing in Publication Data available

Library of Congress Cataloging-in-Publication Data

Chesney, Marion.
  Colonel Sandhurst to the rescue / Marion Chesney.
    p. cm.
  ISBN 0–8161–7415–6 (lg. print : sc)
  1. Large type books.   2. Regency—England—Fiction.
  3. Hotels—England—Fiction.   I. Title.
  [PR6053.H4535C65   1995]
823′.914—dc20   94–17135

For Ann Robinson and
her daughter Emma Wilson,
With love

CHAPTER ONE

There are few ways in which a man can be more innocently employed than in getting money.

—DR. SAMUEL JOHNSON

The poor Relation Hotel in Bond Street, although established only a short time ago by a group of impoverished aristocrats, had come to be accepted by society as if it had always been there.

It was highly successful; the price of staying there was enormous, but it was still less than the horrendous price of hiring a house for the Season, not to mention paying a retinue of servants. The food was famous and the Prince Regent had not only dined there but had attended a charity ball a month before.

And yet, despite this success, not all the partners in the hotel were happy. Colonel Sandhurst, a handsome gentleman in his seventies, longed to marry his partner, the equally elderly Lady Fortescue, and retire to the country. Sir Philip Sommerville, also in his seventies, was in disgrace again, having taken a good part of the money earned from the charity ball and put it on a failure of a horse, and so, feeling guilty, longed to be shot of the hotel and live the life of a gentleman again, forgetting that prior to his involvement in the hotel he had not lived the life of a gentleman for a considerable number of years.

The fourth partner, Miss Letitia Tonks, a spinster in her forties, on the other hand, dreaded the idea of life without the work and companionship the business afforded, and Lady Fortescue, more than any of them, was delighted with their success and had been almost relieved when Sir Philip's folly had meant they would have to work on to secure enough money for a comfortable retirement.

But Sir Philip's dislike of the hotel and everyone in it was demonstrated when they met one evening to discuss finances. There was one outstanding enormous bill, that run up by Sir Randolph Gray and his wife, who had resided in the hotel for six months and had suddenly left, taking even the downy Sir Philip by surprise. What was usual under such circumstances was that Sir Philip would track down whoever owed money and threaten and embarrass them until they paid up.

Lady Fortescue had discovered that Sir Randolph lived in Essex at Barton Park, his country home. She and Colonel Sandhurst were discussing sending Sir Philip off on his debt-collecting mission when Sir Philip, poking his head forward like a tortoise out of his high stiff collar, said, 'Hold on a bit. Why is it always me, hey? Send droopyface here.'

Miss Tonks, correctly interpreting that he

was referring to her, said, 'Debt collecting is a man's job, you old toad,' which showed that the formerly meek and shy spinster had changed a great deal from the days of her poverty, when she had walked along by the Serpentine contemplating suicide.

'Then let Colonel Sandhurst go,' said Sir Philip. 'I'm sick to death of always being the one to get you lot out of fixes.'

'The reason we are in this financial dilemma,' said Lady Fortescue, her black eyes snapping, 'is because you took *our* money and threw it away on a rotten piece of horseflesh.'

'I was only trying to do things for the best,' said Sir Philip. 'I'm not the only one who wastes money. What about her?' He glared balefully at Miss Tonks. 'She's always buying the best seats in the theatre to see that poxy actor, and because she can't go alone she has to take the hotel footman with her.' That 'poxy' actor was a Mr. Jason Davy, who had helped the poor relations in one of their schemes earlier that year. It was one of the delights of Miss Tonks's life to watch him on the stage. She did not have the courage to go backstage and lived in the hope that he might call.

At one time she had nourished hopes that Sir Philip might propose, but now all she could do was dream about the actor. Besides, since the time Sir Philip had been having an affair with a vulgar lady by the name of Mrs. Mary Budge, even the genteel Miss Tonks had come alive to the fact that Sir Philip had certain appetites that might be foreign to a virgin in her forties.

'I will go,' said the colonel, 'so let's have no more squabbling.'

Sir Philip immediately felt at a loss. He liked taking charge, being the one to handle all the difficult matters. 'You'll make a mull of it,' he said nastily.

'I do not think so,' said the colonel. 'Sir Randolph seemed a well-enough gentleman in his way. I do not anticipate any trouble.'

Sir Philip scuttled out. In his heart of hearts, he uncharitably wished Colonel Sandhurst all the worst luck in the world.

*　　*　　*

Colonel Sandhurst was driving a hired carriage. The hotel owners had planned to buy their own carriage, but Sir Philip's loss at the races had put an end to that. The colonel left the hotel at dawn and therefore was confident of arriving at Sir Randolph's late in the afternoon.

But as the distance between himself and Sir Randolph's home shortened, so did his confidence begin to wane. It was all right for the vulgar Sir Philip to be so pushing—*he* had not a sensitive bone in his body—but for a gentleman the collecting of money was highly distasteful.

So, a mile from Sir Randolph's, the colonel

4

drew up at an inn. A little brandy was needed to fortify his spirits.

It was a modest inn, but it was run by a retired army sergeant who recognized in the colonel's manner and bearing an old soldier like himself. He went down to his cellars and brought up a bottle of white brandy that was part of a consignment he had bought from the smugglers. It was very good brandy indeed and it warmed the colonel's heart, as did the flattering attentions of the landlord. When it transpired that the landlord had fought with Sir John Moore at Corunna, the colonel expansively told him to draw up a chair. They fought old battles while the brandy sank lower in the bottle, and it was only the sight of darkness outside the windows that reminded Colonel Sandhurst guiltily of his mission and he rose reluctantly and unsteadily to his feet.

But as he climbed into his carriage after it had been brought round and picked up the reins, he felt a surge of power. He would speak quietly and firmly to Sir Randolph.

The landlord had given him instructions as to how to get to Barton Park, Sir Randolph's home. The colonel's spirits began to plummet as he turned in through the gate posts past a deserted lodge-house and up a long drive. Although it was dark, he could *smell* an estate that had been left to go to seed. And then there was actual physical evidence as unkempt bushes brushed the carriage, and in places the

5

drive was nearly grown over. There was a full moon rising up the sky and suddenly in its silvery light he saw a female figure in front of him on the drive, a figure carrying a bandbox, a figure that let out a startled cry and dived into the bushes.

Had the normally reticent colonel not drunk so much he would have proceeded on his way, but he was anxious to delay the confrontation with Sir Randolph and so he reined in his horses, tethered them to a tree, and plunged into the undergrowth, from which his still sharp ears could hear the sound of muffled sobbing.

Holding high a carriage lamp which he had unhitched, he saw a little clearing ahead of him and there, like Niobe, all tears, perched on the end of a half-shattered ruin of a marble bench, was a young girl. She was holding a wisp of cambric handkerchief to her small nose and sobbing dismally.

'Here now,' said the colonel, advancing. 'This will never do.'

She twisted round and looked up at him. He could see her face clearly in the light of the lamp, which he held high. It was one of the most beautiful and appealing faces he had ever seen, unmarred by her weeping.

'Do not be afraid,' went on the colonel in the same gentle voice. 'I will not harm you.'

'But you will betray me.' A small, choked voice.

'Why not tell me why you are weeping and perhaps I might be of help?' The colonel held out a huge, serviceable handkerchief, which she gratefully took and blew her small nose on.

He put the lantern down on the grass and sat gingerly next to her on the little bit of marble seat that was still intact. She looked at him and studied him and then, perhaps being reassured by his white hair and his years, she said, 'I am running away from home.'

'You are Sir Randolph's daughter?'

'Yes, I am Miss Frederica Gray.'

'And why are you running away from home, Miss Frederica?'

'Papa is forcing me to marry Lord Peter Bewley, a brute of a man and near his dotage. He is forty!'

The colonel gave a little sigh. He himself was in his seventies.

'And how old are you, my child?'

'I am *not* a child. I am seventeen.'

The colonel repressed a smile. 'The age difference between you and Lord Bewley is great, I admit, and yet such arranged marriages often work out very well. You would have your own household, and you would, to a certain extent, know more freedom than you have possibly had before.'

'The man is gross. A brute! I cannot, I won't!'

'But where will you go?'

'I shall walk to the nearest town and catch

7

the stage to London and there I shall find employment as a servant girl.'

The colonel repressed a shudder. He thought of the harridans who waited at the coaching inns in the City to see if they could lure some innocent girl from the country into one of their Covent Garden brothels.

'Who are you? What brings you here?' He realized Frederica was asking him.

'I am part-owner of the Poor Relation Hotel in Bond Street,' said Colonel Sandhurst. 'Sir Randolph left after a long stay and did not pay his bill.'

'He never pays any bills,' said his daughter bitterly. 'When the duns come calling, he sets the dogs on them.'

'Oh.' The colonel looked dismally around the moonwashed glade. He felt all at once deathly sober and it was that feeling which caused his subsequent mad behaviour, for he did not realize that he was still quite tipsy. A great idea sprang into his brain. He would show the others that it was not only Sir Philip who was capable of bold strokes and great cunning. He would offer the girl sanctuary at the hotel. But he would write anonymously to Sir Randolph saying that if he wanted to see his daughter again, he had to pay a certain sum. He, Colonel Sandhurst, would make the sum a little more than the money owing so that Sir Randolph would not suspect the members of the Poor Relation. He stood up. He felt powerful and magnanimous.

'You shall come with me, my dear,' he said, 'and you may stay and work at the hotel and be protected by us until such time as your father comes to his senses.'

Now dry-eyed, she stared up at him, sudden caution in her eyes. 'It is very kind of you, sir, but you do not know me.'

'Lady Fortescue will take care of you. She is a Trojan,' he said.

'Lady Fortescue?'

'The hotel was once her home. She is a very great lady.'

Frederica decided there was something very trustworthy about the elderly colonel. He smelled very strongly of brandy, but in such a hard-drinking age that was not unusual. She gave a little sigh. 'As long as I may earn my keep.'

'In the hotel we all work,' said the colonel. 'You will help Miss Tonks in the rooms when necessary and act as chambermaid.'

Frederica began to brighten by the moment. Having no idea of the work of a servant, although she had been surrounded by a great many of them since the day of her birth, she looked on the prospect of work as something of a game.

'Very well, sir,' she said, getting to her feet. 'I am most indebted to you.'

The colonel took her bandbox and led her back to his carriage.

With a swagger, he tilted his hat at a rakish angle over one eye, picked up the reins and, turning the carriage around, set off at a smart pace, with the small figure of Frederica wrapped in a carriage rug beside him.

*   *   *

Frederica began to feel uneasy when they drew up at a posting-house for the night but was almost immediately reassured when the colonel grandly commanded two of the best bedchambers for himself and his 'niece.'

Over a late supper she told him that she had been ordered to marry Lord Bewley, a man she had never met but had heard about—had heard that he was boorish and, above all, old. The colonel, drinking wine on top of the earlier brandy, smiled indulgently and thought how vastly pretty she was. She was so fine-boned and delicate. Her eyes were wide-spaced and grey, and fringed with thick lashes. She had a soft pink, beautifully shaped mouth, and masses of golden hair, very light, almost silver, with a natural curl. There was a vulnerability about her, a femininity which quickened even his old senses. He thought Sir Randolph was quite mad to throw his daughter away to the first bidder. Had he put her on the market at the Season, she could easily have had her pick. Then he reflected that Sir Randolph probably owed this Lord Bewley money.

The intriguing thing about Frederica was that she was unconscious of her beauty and grace. She switched rapidly between child and woman, at one moment endearingly confiding, at others mature and sensible. The bachelor colonel felt a tug at his heart as he watched and listened to her. Such a girl in the old days would have made an army man a splendid wife. By the time the supper was over, they were chatting like old friends.

'What does your mother say to all this?' asked the colonel.

'Mama does not, and never did, have a say in anything,' said Frederica. 'Papa really wanted a boy and was determined to turn me into one. He taught me to hunt and shoot and fish. Then, just after my seventeenth birthday, one of his friends laughed at him and said, "Don't you know you are looking at the solution to your debts?" And he pointed at me with his riding-crop. It was just after they returned from London. They had not taken me. Suddenly all my breeches were burned and clothes were ordered for me from London and some poor faded lady employed to teach me how to go on in society and a dancing master to teach me to dance. At first it was all very exciting and I was looking forward to the Season I was sure they were preparing me for. I looked forward to meeting girls of my age. Then ... this.'

'And who told you Lord Bewley was such a monster?'

11

'The men on the hunting field used to talk to me as if I were a boy. I heard tales of his womanizing, his hard drinking, oh, all sorts of wicked things.'

'I do not know the man,' said Colonel Sandhurst, 'but I will make it my business to find out. Now, off to bed with you, my dear. We make an early start, and I can assure you, my partners will give you a warm welcome.'

* * *

Late next day, Miss Frederica Gray stood in the staff sitting-room of the Poor Relation Hotel and desperately wished she had never left home. Lady Fortescue was not the comfortable friendly cosy lady Colonel Sandhurst had conjured up. From her delicate lace-cap placed on immaculately coiffed white hair to her snapping black eyes, her high-bridged thin nose, and her straight upright figure, she looked the picture of an autocratic aristocrat. Then there was Sir Philip Sommerville, an old man, small and highly scented, who looked her up and down with pale eyes. Only a spinster lady, Miss Tonks, gave her a sympathetic smile.

'Let us hear this farrago of nonsense again,' said Lady Fortescue.

The colonel was sober, the colonel was miserable, and only the gleam of malicious glee at his discomfiture in Sir Philip's eyes made

12

him stick to his guns. 'I thought it would do no harm to keep Miss Frederica here until Sir Randolph comes to his senses.'

'That was not why you were sent,' said Sir Philip. 'Dear me, it's a case of, if you want a job done, do it yourself.'

The colonel rolled his eyes in the direction of Miss Tonks for help. 'If you could take Miss Frederica next door, Miss Tonks, and help her to unpack and return here, I will explain matters further.' The hoteliers rented an apartment in a building next door to the hotel.

Feeling he needed an ally and sensing one in Miss Tonks, the colonel firmly refused to outline his Great Plan until her return.

When Miss Tonks came in with a cry of 'What a charming and pretty girl!' the colonel found courage to go on. But what had seemed so Machiavellian and clever in a moonlit glade when he was full of brandy seemed quite mad in the sober light of day.

'Let me get this clear,' said Lady Fortescue in a thin voice. 'We are to hold Miss Frederica Gray for ransom, a plan she knows nothing about. What came over you?'

'When I learned he was the type of fellow to set the dogs on me, I thought a visit to him would be futile,' said the colonel stoutly.

'Of all the stupid schemes,' crowed Sir Philip, rubbing his scented little hands.

'Have you a better one, old toad?' demanded Miss Tonks waspishly. 'Are you prepared to

13

face the dogs to get the money? And why do we need the money so desperately? Because of you. Because of your gambling.'

'Be sensible.' Sir Philip's voice cracked with exasperation. 'The minute Sir Randolph gets that note he'll put the Runners on to us.'

'I do not think so,' said the colonel desperately. 'Look here, he's in debt and he wants to market his daughter; he wants to sell her to this Lord Bewley.'

Lady Fortescue's voice was like ice. 'And what happens, pray, if this scheme works? Do we tell that trusting young girl that we were only using her to get money and hand her back to be married to a man she fears?'

The colonel, who had been standing by the fireplace, suddenly sat down and buried his head in his hands.

'I have thought of something,' said Miss Tonks suddenly.

'Hoist the flags, light the lamps, and declare a holiday,' sneered Sir Philip. 'The widgeon has finally had a thought.'

Miss Tonks ignored him. 'We could go ahead with the colonel's plan. The Runners cannot do anything to us. I doubt very much whether Sir Randolph will call them in, for Frederica told me she had left a letter explaining she was running away and why. When Sir Randolph calls with the money, we will tell him that there is a further condition: that Frederica is to have nothing to do with

14

Lord Bewley.'

'And he will stand there and meekly obey our commands?' said Sir Philip.

'We could arrange to meet him, say, in Hyde Park at two in the morning,' said the colonel, taking heart from Miss Tonks's encouragement. 'There are enough of us to spy out the land. At the first sight of a Redbreast, we call the whole thing off. And if the worst comes to the worst, do you think Sir Randolph wants to appear in the newspapers as someone who drove normally honest hotel proprietors to such straits because he did not pay his bill?'

Sir Philip would have gone on opposing the plan if Lady Fortescue had not said, 'There is no answer to our problems but hard work and to keep the hotel for much longer than we had intended.'

The old man stiffened. He was weary of being in trade. The only way to get freedom and get back into polite society was to get Lady Fortescue to sell. It was a mad scheme of the colonel's, but they had done madder things and pulled them off.

'May as well try it,' he said, startling the others with his about-face.

'Has everyone run mad?' asked Lady Fortescue.

Sir Philip gave a horrible sort of conciliatory leer. 'A monster like that deserves to be punished. Hey, I'll even write the letter.'

The colonel looked more relieved by the

15

minute. After all, Sir Philip was used to skulduggery.

'Oh, if you are set on this folly,' exclaimed Lady Fortescue, 'then I must let you all go ahead with it. But do remember that the trusting Miss Frederica must not know of this.'

*　　*　　*

Frederica had placed her small stock of belongings away in the large press in the corner of the room which she was to share with Miss Tonks. She sat on the narrow window-seat and gazed out at the buildings on the other side of Bond Street. She had actually done it! She had escaped and here she was in a safe refuge with these kind hoteliers who only had her best interests at heart. She would work for them as hard as she could. She heaved a little sigh. She had put herself beyond the pale. There could no longer be any dreams of love and marriage. Certainly such dreams had been shattered by her parents' insistence that she marry Lord Bewley, but before that particular axe had fallen, she had often passed the time by imagining the perfect man.

The door opened and Miss Tonks came in, carrying a bolt of print cloth. 'Are you handy with a needle?' asked Miss Tonks.

'I can do plain stitching,' said Frederica doubtfully, 'but I am still not very well versed in ladylike accomplishments.'

16

'Then I will help you. So much more pleasant in our sitting-room next door. The others have gone about their duties.'

An hour later, the gown was cut out and Frederica was stitching busily. She reflected that had she had any friend or sympathetic relative to run to, she would have been plagued by guilt over what she had done. But the surroundings of the hotel were so strange to her, so different from anything she had known, that she could only try to concentrate on the day and forget about the wrath of her father. She was sure he would find her. Until then, she meant to try to enjoy the company of these odd hoteliers as much as possible.

Miss Tonks, working on a sleeve, thought as usual about the actor, Mr. Davy. How she longed to go backstage and see him again. He had called twice at the hotel and taken tea and on both occasions she happened to be absent, shopping over at the milliner's on Ludgate Hill. After hearing of his second visit, she had been frightened to leave the hotel, but he had not called again. But from time to time her thoughts strayed away from Mr. Davy and towards Frederica. The girl was so young, so very pretty, so vulnerable, and so trusting in their goodwill. Miss Tonks shuddered to think how Frederica would react if she learned that she was really being held for ransom.

*   *   *

Lord Bewley strode up and down the Green Saloon in Frederica's home a week later. 'What the deuce were you about, to try forcing the girl into marriage, hey?' he barked. 'I don't want an unwilling bride. Now you say some fiends are holding her to ransom. Let me see that letter again.'

Sir Randolph handed over a piece of parchment. In it Sir Philip had stated bluntly that if Sir Randolph wished to see his daughter again, he must pay eight thousand pounds ransom and deliver it personally to the third oak tree near the west gate at Hyde Park at two in the morning on Friday, the fourteenth of September. If Sir Randolph informed the authorities, his daughter would be killed.

He had not, of course, signed the letter.

'Odd sum,' said Lord Bewley with a scowl. He was a squat, thickset man dressed in plain clothes and top-boots. 'I mean, eight thousand pounds! Why not twenty? They're not to know you are in dun territory.'

'I'm going, and I'm going armed, and I'll shoot whoever turns up,' growled Sir Randolph, 'and I'll give that daughter of mine a whipping when I get her back.'

'So if you shoot whoever,' sneered Lord Bewley, 'how will that get you Frederica back? Why did you not introduce me properly to the girl? One look at me would have put all her fears to rest.' He strode up to the looking-glass and straightened his rather grubby cravat and looked at himself with satisfaction.

'How could I? You've been away in foreign parts.'

'How's Lady Randolph taking it?' asked Lord Bewley.

Sir Randolph looked surprised. A female's feelings were of no account. 'She leaves things to me,' he said.

'As you will leave this business to me,' said Lord Bewley. 'I will go to meet this person or people in Hyde Park. You will pay up, or rather, I will pay the money and add it to the sum you already owe me. As security, I will hold the deeds to your house and estate.'

'What if I cannot pay you?' asked Sir Randolph.

Lord Bewley looked at him in contempt, thinking that, for all his sporting pursuits, Sir Randolph with his padded shoulders and padded calves was a poor figure of a man.

'You'll pay,' he said brutally, 'or you'll lose your house and land. Now what does Frederica look like? Got a miniature?'

But Sir Randolph had not had a miniature taken and shook his head.

'I learn from the county she's a shiner. Yaller hair, big eyes, right?' Sir Randolph nodded his head dumbly and burst into tears. Lord Bewley was unaffected. It was an age when men wept openly and he shrewdly judged that Sir Randolph was weeping over the money he now owed.

'Don't worry,' said Lord Bewley. 'The minute I have your Frederica safe, those villains will wish they had never been born.'

CHAPTER TWO

My valour is certainly going!—it is sneaking off! I feel it oozing out as it were at the palms of my hands!

—SHERIDAN

Sir Philip was in trouble again, trouble which he felt was so unfair considering he had taken over the role of blackmailer. There was an unwritten understanding that Lady Fortescue interviewed and hired female staff and Sir Philip or Colonel Sandhurst hired the male servants. So Lady Fortescue was incensed to learn that Sir Philip had hired a most unsuitable housemaid, one Mary Jones from Shoreditch. It was not that she was bad at her work or that she lacked good references, it was because she was too blonde and buxom, like a milkmaid in a bawdy farce. Her hair was golden and her figure rounded and she appeared just the sort of maid to inflame the passions of the gentlemen guests.

'You know we usually only hire *plain* chambermaids,' said Lady Fortescue crossly. 'That one means trouble, and the only reason you hired her, you old fool, is because you have a roving eye.'

'Brightens up the place,' said Sir Philip defiantly. 'We've enough antidotes as it is.' He flashed a glance at Miss Tonks. Frederica looked up from her sewing. The gown was nearly finished and she was due to start on her duties the following day. 'Besides,' went on Sir Philip, 'we've got Miss Frederica here, and no one in their right mind could call *her* plain.'

'Miss Frederica is protected by her gentility,' said Lady Fortescue. 'Mary has none.'

'She is a good worker and clean,' pointed out Miss Tonks. 'Perhaps the best thing would be to give her a trial.'

'By the end of which time she might be with child,' said Lady Fortescue roundly. 'Now to this other business.'

The colonel flashed her a warning look. 'Frederica,' said Miss Tonks quickly, 'would you be so kind as to go next door and fetch my work-basket? One gown will not suffice, and we had best start cutting out another.'

Frederica obediently left the room.

'Now,' said Lady Fortescue, 'time has passed very quickly, and tomorrow night is when we meet Sir Randolph in Hyde Park. I suggest that Sir Philip and Colonel Sandhurst go and take Jack, the footman, with them.'

The colonel shook his head. 'It won't answer. Jack might gossip. Can't have a servant with us. We'll need to go alone.'

21

Miss Tonks struck an attitude. 'I think we should *all* go. Sir Randolph might be violent, and the presence of ladies may stay his hand.'

'You've been at the playhouse again,' sneered Sir Philip.

'Miss Tonks might have a good point there,' said the colonel, who had been feeling increasingly worried about the whole affair. 'Although I am relieved to see no scandal, no mention in the newspapers of the missing Frederica. But Sir Randolph might simply shoot us. Have you thought of that?'

Miss Tonks emitted a squeak of dismay. Then she said, 'Perhaps we should get in touch with Mr. Davy. Another man...'

'You may as well take out an advertisement and tell the whole of London what we are about,' said Sir Philip. 'Let's keep it in the family. We should not expose the ladies to danger.' He chewed his lip. 'On the other hand, they might add an air of respectability to this mad scheme. Their presence might stop Sir Randolph from resorting to violence.'

'He might feel very violent if, once we have the money, *if* we get the money, we then begin to plead Frederica's case,' said Lady Fortescue. 'And if he insists on taking Frederica home, how do we then explain to the girl how we have betrayed her?'

'I think we will need to cope with all that when the time comes,' said Sir Philip, who felt he did not really care whether Frederica suffered or not. 'We will approach the oak tree cautiously and spy out the land, just in case Sir Philip has brought armed men with him.' He saw the way Miss Tonks's thin hand flew up to her mouth to hide the sudden trembling of her lips and added hurriedly, 'Perhaps it would be best to leave the ladies behind, hey, Colonel?'

But Lady Fortescue said with a little sigh, 'At my age, I am not frightened of death. Miss Tonks may wait here for us.'

'No, if you are going, then I will go, too,' said Miss Tonks with a bravery she did not feel. 'Hush, I think I hear Frederica returning.'

Frederica came in, her cheeks pink and her eyes shining. But she did not say anything, merely picking up her sewing and bending her head over it. Frederica had no intention of telling her new friends that she had met Romance slap-bang in the middle of Bond Street.

*   *   *

She had flown out of the hotel and had collided with a tall gentleman. 'Steady, miss,' he had said in an amused voice. 'You will do us both an injury running about like that.'

Confused, Frederica had backed off and dropped a curtsy and then looked up into his face.

He had swept off his hat and made a low bow. 'Captain Peter Manners of the Guards, at

23

your service,' he said.

He was very tall, with black curly hair and wicked blue eyes, a strong chin and a tanned face.

'I am Miss Frederica ... er ... Black,' said Frederica, 'and I am most sorry I stumbled into you, sir.'

'My pleasure, I assure you,' he said in a pleasant light drawl. His eyes took in her simple but expensive gown. 'You should not be unescorted in Bond Street, Miss ... er ... Black.'

'I am only going next door where I have a room,' said Frederica. 'I ... work at the hotel.'

She bobbed another curtsy and ran off up a narrow dark stair next to the hotel.

He stood stock-still for a few moments. She was too well-gowned and too well-spoken to be a servant. Perhaps she was a lady's-maid to one of the guests. But then she would have said so. Then the Poor Relation was famous for being staffed by members of the quality. He himself was staying at Limmer's, enjoying his leave from the army. He should have been staying with his widowed mother in Berkeley Square but he had pleaded with her that as he would be entertaining many army friends, it was better he should be at Limmer's Hotel, home of the Corinthian set, rather than cluttering up her drawing-room with noisy bucks. The fact that his fiancée and her mother were residing with Lady Manners, his mother, was a thought he refused to acknowledge. He had proposed to Belinda Devenham on his last leave because she had been presented to him as a suitable bride, because he thought he would never fall in love, because war had made him anxious for a certain stability in his otherwise rackety life. But at the end of his last leave it had been borne in on him that the fair Belinda disapproved of him and meant to reshape him in her own image, which was of all that was the most respectable. He had thought of her often while he had been away and each thought had made him uneasy. The fact that his mother had written to him shortly before his arrival in London to inform him that Mrs. Devenham and her daughter were staying with her had made him realize the wisdom of staying at Limmer's Hotel, although he would not admit the real reason to himself.

He strolled along to Limmer's and went into the coffee room. His friend, another captain, Jack Warren, hailed him.

'How goes the world?'

Captain Manners sat down and smiled at his friend. 'Surprising well. I collided with the most beautiful creature I have ever seen outside the Poor Relation.'

'You're engaged to be married,' said Jack. 'Take me along and introduce me.'

'She said she was a servant,' said Captain Manners, half to himself. 'She said her name was Miss Frederica ... er ... Black. I noted the

25

"er." I do not think her name is really Black. She was too well-dressed and well-spoken to be a servant.'

'The same could be said for any of that terrifying lot who run the hotel,' said Jack with feeling. 'Went there for dinner one night and felt I had strayed into a ton party to which I had not been invited. Devilish steep prices, too. Perhaps I might take a stroll along to their coffee room and see if I can see your fair charmer.'

Jack Warren was a tall, thin Irishman of no particular looks but a great deal of charm. Captain Manners felt a sudden stab of irritation. He looked up to find a footman holding out a note. The footman was wearing the Manners' livery.

He scanned the note. His mother, reminding him that he was expected to call.

He got to his feet. 'I must go,' he said. 'I think that the beautiful miss does not work at that hotel. I think she was lying. No point in wasting your time at such an expensive place looking for her.'

He walked moodily to Berkeley Square. Gunter's, the confectioner's at the corner of the square, was doing good business. Two young men were leaving. They looked happy. They were probably not engaged to be married, he thought sourly and then flinched at that first disloyal thought, or the first disloyal thought that he had allowed to formulate

26

clearly in his mind.

He walked up the shallow steps to his mother's door. It was a sunny day. The plane trees in Berkeley Square, planted the same year as the French Revolution, were turning colour, and there was an invigorating nip of early-autumn cold in the air. The butler opened the door to him. Captain Manners walked into the dark hall. He heard the door close behind him and he felt he had entered prison.

'My lady is in the drawing-room with Mrs. and Miss Devenham,' said the butler.

The captain reluctantly surrendered his hat, gloves, and stick and walked slowly up the stairs.

He paused in the doorway of the drawing-room as the butler announced him. Then he walked forward and kissed his mother on her powdery cheek before turning to the other two ladies. He felt a sensation of relief when he saw Belinda. She was graceful, with thick reddish-brown hair piled up on her head exposing her long white neck. Her eyes were very full and liquid, and only the most carping critic might have remarked that they were a trifle protruding. She was twenty-two years old but the captain was thirty-one, and had been assured that Belinda's unwed state was because her fastidious mind had not allowed her to accept any of the many proposals of marriage she had already received. He thought she looked very well in a pretty white muslin gown with many flounces and little puffed sleeves. She had an excellent bosom and was flattered by the current high-waisted styles, for she was a trifle thick about the real waistline, which the latest fashions disguised. She did not smile at him, being well brought up and knowing that any excess of emotion was unladylike. She held out her hand and he kissed the air somewhere above it. 'We are pleased to see you,' she remarked calmly. Her mother, a small squat toad of a woman, said, 'Where have you been?'

'I explained to Mother that I have been entertaining army friends at Limmer's,' said the captain. 'Good fellows but not suitable for a lady's drawing-room.'

Mrs. Devenham gave a little grunt and then said, 'Belinda, get your portfolio and show the captain your water-colours. They are amazing fine.'

Belinda fetched a portfolio and opened it up on a round table in the centre of the room. He realized that she rarely sat down. He stood beside her as she extracted one water-colour after another. They were competently executed but, he thought, very dull. He admired each one. There seemed to be a great many. He stifled a yawn and racked his brain for something new and complimentary to say about each.

His initial feeling of relief at the handsome appearance presented by his fiancée was rapidly evaporating. He remembered, with a startling vividness which surprised him, a beautiful face gazing up into his outside the Poor Relation Hotel in Bond Street.

*　　*　　*

Frederica shared a bed with Miss Tonks. Miss Tonks had a bad habit of sleeping on her back and snoring, and so, relieved to find the spinster intended to stay up late the following night, Frederica composed herself quickly for sleep, hoping that she could drop off before Miss Tonks arrived. But the harsh cry of the watch calling the half-hour awoke her and she realized she was still alone. All at once she felt wide awake and restless. She lit the candle by the bed and peered at the clock. Half past one! She climbed out of bed and went to the window, opened it, and looked out. She heard furtive noises from the street below and, curious, Frederica leaned farther out. A carriage was drawn up outside the hotel entrance. Sir Philip, Lady Fortescue, Colonel Sandhurst, and Miss Tonks were standing beside it. As she watched, Miss Tonks drew a pistol from her reticule and said in a clear voice, 'Yes, it is primed and ready,' before she was shushed into silence by the others. Then the colonel climbed on the box while the others got inside, and the carriage moved off.

Frederica rubbed her bare arms, feeling suddenly cold. She closed the window and retreated to the bed. How odd! How frightening. What did she really know of these people? Respectable people did not go out in the dead of night armed with pistols unless they were going on a long journey, and the carriage had been an open one, suitable for short drives to the Park, but hardly the equipage for any significant expedition.

She began to wonder whether she had jumped out of the frying-pan into the fire, whether Lord Bewley might not be so terrifying as her new protectors.

*   *   *

Lord Bewley stood under the oak tree. Cowardice was not one of his many faults. He felt quite calm. He planned to hand over the money *after* they had produced Frederica. The letter written to Sir Randolph had been that of an educated man. He had no fear of being set upon by footpads. He expected them to be masked. He wondered why they had chosen this particular night, for the full moon was shining brightly.

He heard a carriage approaching and took a serviceable pistol out of his pocket and held it at the ready.

He cocked his head to one side. The carriage had stopped. Several people, to judge by the sounds. He considered his situation. Perhaps they would kill him. If they were not masked,

30

they surely would expect him to expose them. But instead of being frightened, he felt light-headed and reckless.

He stepped out boldly from the shadow of the tree and then stood stock-still. Two elderly gentlemen, one elderly lady, and one lady of uncertain years stood clearly revealed by the moonlight. His first thought was that some elderly eccentrics had decided to go for a walk in the Park in the dead of night. He looked past them. He looked all about him.

'You,' said Lady Fortescue clearly, 'are not Sir Randolph.'

'I am Lord Bewley, at your service.' He walked up to them. 'Never tell me that you are the kidnappers.'

'Have you the money?' demanded Sir Philip, always one to get to the point.

'I have the ransom money with me. Where is Miss Frederica?'

'Safe and well,' said the colonel.

'Now look here, you odd lot,' said Lord Bewley, stuffing his pistol into his pocket, 'you can't expect me to pay anything until I have seen her. Who are you anyway? You're the oddest bunch of criminals I've ever seen.'

'You hand over that money,' said Sir Philip, 'or you'll never see Frederica again.'

'No girl, no money,' said Lord Bewley, beginning to sound amused.

'This is hopeless,' said Sir Philip. 'What a stupid idea.'

31

'I think in this case, only the truth will serve,' said Lady Fortescue. 'The facts are these, Lord Bewley. Miss Frederica ran away from home to escape marriage to you. We gave her refuge. Sir Randolph owes us a great deal of money and we saw a way to recoup it.'

The moon, which had gone behind a cloud, suddenly shone down again full on Colonel Sandhurst's face.

'Wait a bit,' said Lord Bewley, peering at him. 'I know you. You're that Colonel Sandhurst. The Poor Relation Hotel. That's it! You're that lot.'

'Sir Randolph did not pay his bill. He stayed with us with his wife for six months,' said Lady Fortescue. 'He entertained friends. His bill came to nearly four thousand pounds. We are demanding eight thousand to cover that bill and punish him for putting us to this trouble. Frederica is at the hotel. She does not know of this plan. You must take our word for it that she is safe and well. But you must forgo all plans of marrying her. You are too old.'

'How can anyone in this day and age run up a hotel bill of four thousand pounds?' demanded Lord Bewley.

'On one occasion,' said Lady Fortescue evenly, 'he gave a dinner for fifty guests, with presents for all.'

'And you let him get away with it? Amateurs.'

'It is the only occasion on which we have

32

been tricked out of so much,' said Sir Philip wrathfully. 'We are used to people running up huge bills. You know how it is. I doubt if you have even paid your own tailor this age.'

'I pay my bills,' said Lord Bewley. He stood, legs apart, a powerful John Bull sort of figure.

'So Frederica is hidden away in your hotel.'

'Not exactly *hidden*,' said Miss Tonks, speaking for the first time. 'We all work. She will help as a chambermaid until her father comes to his senses.'

Lord Bewley thought hard. He had to confess he was now relieved that he had had to face not a gang of thugs but this farcical foursome. The whole situation began to amuse him greatly. He did not like Sir Randolph. He himself did not stand to lose anything, for he could claim Sir Randolph's house and lands anytime he chose and Sir Randolph was surely not going to lose everything over such a small debt—the debt being small to Lord Bewley in an age when men could lose considerably more than that over the gaming tables of St. James's.

'So if I go along with this scheme,' he said, 'do I return and tell Sir Randolph that I have paid over good money and that his daughter is still missing?'

'What you can tell him,' said Sir Philip, 'is that Frederica is safe and well. You have our word for that. We will get her to write a letter to her parents, saying that she is staying with a respectable family.'

'But what if I want to marry her?' asked Lord Bewley. 'Thought of that, hey?'

'I gather you have never seen her,' said Lady Fortescue. 'A fine-looking man like yourself,' she added mendaciously, 'can surely get any lady he wants without bothering over some flighty chit of a schoolgirl.'

'True,' remarked his lordship complacently. 'Tell you what I'll do. I'll give you the money, but only what Sir Randolph owed. That's fair.'

'I think,' said the colonel cautiously, 'that we should accept Lord Bewley's offer.' Lord Bewley counted out the money in notes. Miss Tonks gave a little gulp of relief. But her relief died the moment the transaction was over, when Lord Bewley said, 'I may as well move into that hotel of yours. Town house is in need of repair.'

'But Frederica must not meet you!' squeaked Miss Tonks.

'I'm not supposed to know she's working as a chambermaid, and if truth be told, after the way she's behaved, I have no interest at all in the girl. *I* won't say I know her.'

Gratitude that they were all still alive, that he had not shot them or called the Runners, that he had proved to be so amiable made the hoteliers agree he could stay at the hotel. And, as Lady Fortescue whispered to the colonel, other work would be found for Frederica. She need never meet Lord Bewley.

Frederica was summoned to the sitting-room the following day, where she was alarmed to learn that Lord Bewley, whom she had left home to escape, was now resident at the hotel.

'There is no reason to be afraid,' said Lady Fortescue. 'He knows you are here, for we met him by chance last night and decided to be honest with him. He will not betray you. He does not want to marry you but we feel that if you return home, your father might try to persuade Lord Bewley to change his mind. So we suggest you write a letter to your parents, not telling them your direction, but saying you are living with a respectable family and will write again soon.'

A stab of guilt at her own behavior hit Frederica. She remembered that odd expedition last night, Miss Tonks with the pistol. What did she really know of these new friends? She should return home and beg forgiveness. Had they *threatened* Lord Bewley? But then, he would hardly be a guest at the hotel if they had. And then she saw the handsome face of that army man she had collided with in Bond Street. Somewhere out there in busy London he was to be found. If she returned to the country she would never see him again.

So she said, 'I will write the letter. But if I am to work as a chambermaid, I will meet Lord

Bewley and I do not wish to do that.'

'As to that,' said Lady Fortescue, 'I have decided to put you to work in the kitchens, for only a short time each day. Despard, our chef, is a genius, but temperamental. His underchef, Rossignole, is the easier of the two. He will introduce you to the arts of cooking, something every lady should know. I do not hold with the current generation who brag that they never set foot in their own kitchens. Miss Tonks will introduce you.' Miss Tonks quailed. She was frightened of both Despard and Rossignole because they were both French and everyone knew the French ate babies roasted for breakfast. The fact that this idea was illogical, that one roasted baby on the premises of the Poor Relation Hotel would cause one of the worst scandals of the century, did not occur to her. The British had been at war with the French for so long that even the middle-aged Miss Tonks had been brought up on horror stories of what they were capable of doing.

'No time like the present,' said Sir Philip maliciously, for he knew Miss Tonks was afraid of the chef. 'Why not take Frederica down and introduce her?'

'Very well.' Miss Tonks threw him a look of loathing. 'Come along, my dear.'

Despard and Rossignole were seated at the kitchen table sharing a bottle of wine and resting from their labours.

'This is Frederica,' said Miss Tonks bravely. 'Lady Fortescue wishes her to help for a short time each day in the kitchen and she is to be instructed in the art of cooking.'

Frederica stood nervously behind Miss Tonks. Despard's white and twisted face assumed an uglier aspect as he sneered, 'I have no time for useless females in my kitchen.'

'It is not *your* kitchen,' said Miss Tonks in a trembling voice. 'It is *our* kitchen.'

Frederica stepped out from behind Miss Tonks. She was wearing one of her own gowns, a pretty white muslin. A shaft of sunlight from the dingy window up at street level shone on her hair, on her wide eyes, on the exquisite and delicate beauty of her face.

'Ma foi!' said Rossignole under his breath. He stood up, as did Despard, and both tugged off their skull-caps. 'There is no need to be so rude to Miss Tonks,' said Frederica in a clear voice.

'We get cross and crusty in our work,' said Despard, drawing out a chair, his voice its usual mixture of French and Cockney accents. 'Sit down! I myself shall instruct you in my arts. A glass of wine, miss?'

Miss Tonks, finding herself ignored, gratefully left the kitchen. She stood outside the green baize door and leaned her narrow back against it. Beauty, that was the charm which unlocked all hearts. She envied Frederica. In that moment, she wished she

37

looked like Frederica so that Mr. Jason Davy would consider her to be more than a friend. With a little sigh she made her way upstairs to the main hall.

The hall was empty apart from a tall gentleman pacing up and down under the chandelier which, despite the sunlight outside, was burning brightly with many candles, for the hall was dark and Sir Philip had rightly pointed out that the magnificent Waterford chandelier was an advertisement in itself.

'May I help you, sir?' asked Miss Tonks.

He smiled down at her and she blinked rapidly and nervously, feeling she had had enough of beauty for one day, for his face was handsome and his smile blinding in its charm.

'I collided with a servant girl from this hotel, a Miss Frederica Black. I am called to make sure she came to no harm,' said Captain Manners.

'I know of no Miss Black,' said Miss Tonks, and the captain's heart sank. 'Can you describe her?' added Miss Tonks.

'Hair like gold, vastly pretty, grey eyes, young.'

Our Frederica, thought Miss Tonks, but what am I to do? Life is complicated enough. So she shook her head. 'I am sorry I cannot help you, sir.'

The captain bowed and left. How dingy and dull London now seemed!

38

*   *   *

Lord Bewley, established in the Poor Relation, awoke early and lay tingling with anticipation. This Frederica would no doubt come in and draw the curtains and leave his morning cup of chocolate beside the bed. He was sure his (in his opinion) masculine good looks would win her over.

The door opened and a female figure entered the shadowy room. He waited until he heard a light step, the chink of china beside the bed and then the scrape of the brass curtain rings. He sat up and blinked in awe. Surely there had never been a fairer creature. Her hair was pure gold, her figure like that of Venus, her eyes a deep, deep blue. He was stunned. He was speechless. She dropped him a curtsy and quietly left the room.

He had to have her! But he would not let anyone know. No coercion. He would woo her as he had never wooed a woman before.

Mary Jones, chambermaid, went into the servants' hall. 'Who's the codger in the Red Room?' she asked.

'Lord Bewley,' said Jack, the footman.

She gave a slow smile and then giggled. 'Strange-looking fellow,' she said. 'He kept gawping at me.'

CHAPTER THREE

Of all the torments, all the cares,
With which our lives are curst;
Of all the plagues a lover bears,
Sure rivals are the worst!
By partners, in each other kind,
Afflictions easier grow;
In love alone we hate to find
Companions of our woe.
—WILLIAM WALSH

Sir Philip Sommerville felt there was something strange about Miss Tonks. Although they often clashed, he had been aware before of the spinster's regard for him and, yes, he had been also aware of her hopes of marriage to him. But of late, she had avoided his company. Piqued and driven to consideration for her feelings at last, he had gruffly invited her to Gunter's for tea, but instead of her eyes shining with suitable gratitude, she had said quietly that she was busy and had gone quickly away.

Miss Tonks was worried. The production in which Mr. Davy had been appearing had closed and she could not see his name anywhere on the playbills. She had at first assumed that he might be touring the provinces, but surely he would have gone with the same company and *they* were opening in a new play and Mr. Davy's name was nowhere to be seen.

Desperate feelings demanded desperate measures. Colonel Sandhurst had told her about the coffee-house in Covent Garden frequented by actors, where he had first met Mr. Davy. Knowing she could not go there on her own, she had begged Jack, the footman, to accompany her, but Jack had been warned by Sir Philip not to indulge the spinster's pursuit of some 'mountebank of an actor' and so he had said his duties at the hotel did not permit it, adding that he had work to do for Sir Philip, but if madam liked to ask Sir Philip ...? And, of course, madam did not.

And then she hit on a plan. She had dressed as a man before when she had pretended to be a highwayman. Well, with great daring, she would dress as a man again and go to that coffee shop and see if there was any news of Mr. Davy. Not wanting to be too profligate, she hired, rather than bought, a suit of men's clothes, saying that she was going to take part in amateur theatricals. Now in the romances Miss Tonks loved to read, the heroine sometimes dressed as a man and the hero never even recognized his beloved. But Miss Tonks in men's clothes still looked exactly like Miss Tonks, and furthermore, she did not look at all like a man despite her thin, flat-chested figure, for she carried about with her an air of genteel femininity. But she *felt* different, very swaggering and adventurous. She managed to slip out of the staff apartment next door without being seen and strode along the London streets feeling very bold and daring.

It was an age when women often dressed in men's clothes and sometimes even enlisted in the military, quite a number of them taking the secret of their sex to the grave. But these were women who looked like men.

Mr. Davy, seated in a dark corner, looked up as he heard the whispers and sniggers. He peered across at the doorway and blinked. Miss Tonks was standing there looking about her with a tentative, sheepish smile. She was wearing a blue coat, knee-breeches, and clocked stockings. She had an excellent pair of legs, however, and it was these limbs which were becoming the increasing focus of ribald comment.

The actor rose quickly to his feet and tossed some coins on the table. He hurried to join her and, putting a hand under her elbow, he steered her out into the street. 'Miss Tonks,' he said urgently, 'my lodgings are hard by. It may go against the conventions to take you there, but you should not be abroad in such disgraceful clothes.' Miss Tonks blushed miserably. 'You recognized me!'

'Of course,' he said quietly.

'But I am dressed as a *man*.'

'No clothes could make you look like a man,

Miss Tonks,' he said, laughter lighting up his eyes. Mr. Davy was a slightly built middle-aged man whose thick brown hair was lightly dusted with grey. He could, in fact, pass unnoticed in any crowd, but to Miss Tonks he was the most handsome man in London.

He escorted her round the corner and up a dingy wooden staircase to a scarred door which he unlocked. 'My quarters are a poor affair,' he said apologetically, 'but actors are never famous for spending much money on living accommodations.'

Miss Tonks looked around. There was a living-room with some battered furniture. A door opened off it to reveal a bedroom with an unmade bed. Mr. Davy closed the bedroom door and then put the kettle on the fire. 'We shall have a glass of the out-of-work actor's drink,' he said cheerfully. 'Gin and hot.'

Sitting gingerly on the very edge of an armchair as he put a blackened kettle on the glowing embers of the fire, Miss Tonks felt very gauche and shy.

'Now,' said Mr. Davy, sitting down opposite her, 'you must tell me why you came in search of me in such a guise. I assume you *did* come in search of me?'

Miss Tonks nodded. 'I could not see your name anywhere in the theatres and ... and ... I became worried ... and ... and ... I could not go on my own dressed as a woman or tell anyone where I was going.' She shifted her thin bottom awkwardly. 'How do you go on?'

'Tolerable well. But I fell foul of the theatre manager. I accused him of cheating at cards. A silly thing to do, for any actor should know by now to pay and keep quiet.'

Miss Tonks had been brought up to believe that a lady never discussed money. But life in the hotel business had changed all that. She gave a little cough and asked tentatively, 'Are you in funds?'

He gave her a wry look from his brown eyes. 'In a job where playing cards with the manager who cheats is part of the deal, it is not a very lucrative profession. I must shortly look around for some employ.'

'What will you do?'

'Perhaps be a porter in Covent Garden Market.'

'Oh, no! You are a gentleman.'

'I am not a gentleman, Miss Tonks, which means I can work at anything I please.'

He rose and poured two measures of gin from a squat bottle and then, seeing that the kettle was steaming, added hot water.

'Your health,' he said, raising his glass after handing her the other one. 'No heeltaps!'

'No heeltaps,' echoed Miss Tonks, marvelling at how her dreary spinsterish life had changed so much that she should be sitting in an actor's flat in Covent Garden drinking hot gin with him.

'It is not very pleasant being poor,' she said.

44

'I do not know what I would have done had not Lady Fortescue and Colonel Sandhurst rescued me. I was walking by the Serpentine feeling wretched and hungry and I did not even have the courage to throw myself in.' Her voice became dreamy. 'Such a mad idea, that a few poor relations should band together for survival. And then Sir Philip's idea about starting the hotel.' Her eyes suddenly glowed. 'Why, *you* could join us. I am sure Colonel Sandhurst would be pleased.'

He shook his head. 'You forget I was brought to the hotel initially to wean Sir Philip away from that horrible woman he was threatening to marry. It would not answer.'

But once she had grasped hold of the wonderful thought that there might be a way to keep this man where she could see him every day, Miss Tonks was not going to change her mind.

'Come with me now,' she urged. 'We could approach Colonel Sandhurst first, and Lady Fortescue. If they say yes, and I most certainly do, then Sir Philip cannot have any say in the matter.'

'But what could I *do*?' he demanded, half exasperated.

Her brain activated by the unaccustomed gin, Miss Tonks beamed. 'You could be our debt collector. Sir Philip often does it, but he does not like it and the colonel hates asking people for money. It is not only the guests who sometimes slip off without paying, but the guests who come for dinner of an evening or even visitors to the coffee room. They often say they have left their money at home and we take them on trust because one does that in our trade,' added Miss Tonks earnestly.

'I could do that,' he said slowly. 'My profession has given me a very thick hide. I enjoyed my stay at the Poor Relation.'

'Come this evening after dinner,' urged Miss Tonks.

He smiled and shrugged. 'Why not? Worth a try. Have some more gin.' And Miss Tonks smiled at him dreamily and held out her glass.

*   *   *

Frederica was in the room she shared with Miss Tonks changing into a clean gown. She had enjoyed her lessons in the kitchen and had been allowed to help with the dinner preparations. The satisfaction of actually doing some work had temporarily put the handsome face of that captain to the back of her mind. And yet he was still there, which was why she changed into one of the nicest of her few gowns. There was always the hope, not quite admitted to herself, that when she left the apartment to walk to the hotel next door, he might be there, on the street, just passing.

She gave a final pat to her hair and left the room just in time to see a shadowy figure dart

46

for cover round the L of the corridor. 'Who's there?' she called.

There was no reply. The apartment house was silent. Muffled traffic sounds filtered up from Bond Street: the grating of brewers' sledges, the rumbling of coaches, the sounds of horses' hooves.

'Who's there?' she called again, sharply this time.

Again no reply, but Frederica sensed someone was there waiting. The staircase was temptingly between her and the end of the corridor and she scampered down it. But she stopped at the bottom. The work she had done in the kitchens had given her a feeling of bravery, of independence. She felt it was her duty to see if she could find out who it was at the top of the stairs.

She crept quietly back up, her thin, flat-heeled leather shoes making no sound.

She heard a furtive grating of a key being turned in a lock. She remembered she had locked the room door behind her. She gained the top of the stairs and peered round. Miss Tonks, dressed in a suit of men's clothes, had just unlocked the door of the room she shared with Frederica and was slipping quietly inside.

Frederica sat down suddenly on the top step, her heart hammering. How odd! Who was Miss Tonks, really? Who was this genteel lady who could prime a pistol and who wandered the daylight streets of London disguised as a man? She wanted to talk to someone about it but was afraid to do so. What if these hoteliers were involved in black deeds? It was all very strange. Life had become strange. Although she had scanned the newspapers, there was no news of her disappearance and she had been sure her father would have alerted the Runners to find her and bring her home.

She got up, noticing that her knees trembled a little and that she was not nearly as brave as she thought she had become, and went back downstairs and out into the busy street. She was so upset about the strange behaviour of Miss Tonks that she did not notice the handsome captain on the other side of the street who stopped short at the sight of her. Captain Peter Manners tried to cross the street quickly but traffic was flowing briskly in both directions. He dived round a chaise and got roundly cursed by the driver. But when he reached the Poor Relation Hotel, there was no sign of her.

He walked thoughtfully towards Limmer's. There was no reason why he himself could not stay at the Poor Relation. He had plenty of money. He did not stop to think of his engagement. He only felt relieved that he had decided on a course of action—that, if he got to know this pretty girl, he would find she was a common servant, nothing out of the ordinary, and so get the wretched female out of his head for once and for all.

Miss Tonks had not found the courage to tell the others about Mr. Davy. After the dinner was over and she knew they would gather in the sitting-room at the top of the hotel and that Mr. Davy would join them there, she began to feel increasingly nervous, almost beginning to hear Sir Philip's gibes ringing in her ears.

But fear kept her quiet. She took her customary chair in the sitting-room, looking nervously at the door and starting at every sound. Frederica was sewing quietly in a corner. So nervous was Miss Tonks that at first she did not realize that the discussion which was going on was to her—and Mr. Davy's—advantage.

'Lord Braby,' Sir Philip was saying, 'hired us to cater for his daughter's come-out last Season and so far has not paid us for our services. Why was this overlooked?'

'You are the one who overlooked it,' said Lady Fortescue tartly. 'You keep the books, although I must say that after your disgraceful behaviour on the racecourse, where you lost *our* money, it would be more intelligent to give the bookkeeping duties back to Miss Tonks.'

'She can't add two and two.'

'That is untrue,' declared Miss Tonks, becoming alive to the situation.

'Miss Tonks was very competent,' said the colonel.

'Forget about Miss Tonks,' said Sir Philip brutally. 'Who is going to call on Lord Braby?'

'He has a short way with duns, or so I have heard,' said the colonel meditatively. 'Besides, he's not in Town. He's at his place in Sussex.'

'He's back.' Sir Philip's eyes gleamed with malice. He knew the colonel was dreading being asked to go and collect the money, and although he himself was not looking forward much to the prospect, he was jealous of the colonel and liked to see him out of sorts.

The door opened and Mr. Davy walked in.

'My dear fellow!' cried the colonel, jumping to his feet. 'Welcome! Some claret? Despard has found us some fine wine. One hopes he has not been consorting with the smugglers, but that seems to be the only way one gets decent wine these days.'

Frederica noticed that although Lady Fortescue was also pleased to see this newcomer, Miss Tonks blushed red and Sir Philip was glaring at her.

Mr. Davy, glass in hand, sat down and beamed around. 'So what is your decision?' he asked.

'What decision?' Lady Fortescue's thin eyebrows rose in surprise.

'Did not Miss Tonks tell you?'

All looked at Miss Tonks, who began to stammer, 'There h-hasn't r-really been any t-time.'

'What have you been up to, you silly

widgeon?' demanded Sir Philip.

Mr. Davy threw the agonized spinster a sympathetic look. 'I am out of work at the moment,' he said pleasantly. 'Miss Tonks was kind enough to suggest I might join forces with you.'

'What!' Sir Philip stared at him wrathfully. 'We are no longer poor, sir, as you very well know, and not in the way of taking charity cases.'

Frederica winced and the colonel said heavily, 'Mind your manners, sir!'

'I suggested he might collect debts for us,' said Miss Tonks. '*You* don't want to do it, Colonel, and I do not believe you enjoy it either, Sir Philip.'

Sir Philip opened his mouth to rage and then suddenly shut it again. There had been a report in a newspaper of Lord Braby's horsewhipping a dun. His eyes began to gleam with malicious delight and he leaned back in his chair and said expansively, 'Now that's different. We do have a pressing debt outstanding. I suggest we give Mr. Davy here a trial.'

'I must admit it would be comforting to have another gentleman to help us with our problems,' said Lady Fortescue, and Colonel Sandhurst shot a jealous look at Mr. Davy.

'I told Miss Tonks this afternoon that I had lost a great deal of money by being forced to gamble with my cheating employer,' said Mr. Davy, 'but I still have by me a certain sum

51

which I will gladly put into the hotel.'

Sir Philip's lips parted in a thin smile. 'Dear fellow, we are not much interested in pennies. How much?'

'About five hundred pounds.'

'How on earth can an actor accumulate that much?'

'You forget I played the lead,' said Mr. Davy, 'and there is good money to be earned in provincial tours. I have always saved money by living simply. I was in desperate straits when the colonel found me the last time and I never want to have to endure such poverty or hunger again.'

'But you live so shabbily,' exclaimed Miss Tonks. 'And this afternoon at your lodgings, you said because you were out of funds, you would perhaps have to find work as a porter in the market.'

'I did not intend to touch my capital. I am beginning to save for my old age,' said Mr. Davy. 'I did not mean to mislead you, Miss Tonks.'

Lady Fortescue's black eyes snapped with curiosity. 'Do I understand from these interesting revelations that our Miss Tonks visited you at your *lodgings*?'

'I was dressed as a man,' said Miss Tonks simply. 'There was no scandal.'

Frederica looked up and suddenly smiled in relief. What a simple explanation. Nothing sinister at all. But it was evident that Lady

Fortescue was deeply shocked.

'Miss Tonks,' she said awfully, 'although we have all sunk to trade—'

'With the exception of our friend here'—Sir Philip nodded in the direction of Mr. Davy—'who has *risen* in the world by association with us.'

'As I was saying before I was so very rudely interrupted,' went on Lady Fortescue, 'we must continue to present a highly respectable profile to the world. What will Miss Frederica think of such a poor example as you, Miss Tonks? Fie, for shame.'

'I was very grateful to her,' said Mr. Davy quietly. 'I was feeling very lost and lonely and unwanted.'

Miss Tonks, who had bent her head under Lady Fortescue's attack, continued to look down, but only to hide from the rest the sudden joy in her eyes.

'It is agreed, then' said Lady Fortescue, looking around, 'that it would be only fair to give Mr. Davy a trial before we take his money?'

There was a murmur of agreement.

'Well, then,' said the colonel, who could never remain out of sorts for long, 'now you are with us, Mr. Davy, all that remains for you is to bring your belongings to us tomorrow, but in the meantime, we would love to hear one of your songs.'

To Frederica's delight, Mr. Davy

53

entertained them with ballads while the claret and tea circulated. She felt she was part of a family circle for the first time. But there was a bigger delight in store for her.

When Mr. Davy had left and Miss Tonks was indicating to her that it was time they retired, Sir Philip said suddenly, 'I let the Yellow Room.'

'Oh, good,' said Lady Fortescue. 'A most difficult room to find a customer for, considering it is so small and dark. Who has taken it?'

'A Captain Peter Manners.'

Miss Tonks saw the sudden flush of delight on Frederica's expressive face and gave a little sigh.

More complications!

* * *

Lord Bewley awoke the next morning and lay tingling with expectation. He heard the door softly open, smelt hot chocolate, and then felt the light on his face as the curtains were drawn back. He sat up, affecting to come awake, although he had already been awake for some time. Mary Jones dropped a curtsy. 'A fine day, my lord,' she said, 'but with a chill in the air.'

'You must have been out already,' said his lordship admiringly, 'for it has brought a good colour to your cheeks. I like a girl with a bit of colour.'

Mary giggled. 'Go on with you.'

'You do that very well,' commented Lord Bewley.

'What is that, my lord?'

'Your accent.'

'Thank you, my lord.' Mary dropped another curtsy. 'It's a great step up in the world for the likes of me to work here, so I try to speak like the ladies.'

To her surprise, this eccentric lord laughed heartily. 'You should ha' gone on the stage,' he chuckled. 'I say, do this lot give you any time off?'

'I am supposed to get an evening or afternoon free when the hotel is not busy, my lord, but there's few times like that.' She stood by the window, the sunlight on her blonde hair and the curves of her buxom figure silhouetted by the light. Lord Bewley's mouth was suddenly dry.

'Take you out one evening,' he said gruffly.

She coloured. 'T'would not be fitting, my lord. I mean, me and a great gennelman like yourself.'

Once more he was amazed at the brilliance of what he believed to be her play-acting. 'No one would need to know,' he said quickly. 'Tell you what. Take you to Astley's.'

Astley's Amphitheatre on the south side of the river was famous for its dramatic plays and exciting spectacles. Mary looked at him, her mouth a little open. Then she said, 'I've always dreamt of going there.'

'Hey, so what about it?'

She hesitated. 'I would need to ask my employers.'

He scowled suddenly. He could point out to these freaks who ran the hotel that he had every right to take Frederica out with him, that the girl wanted to go. But perhaps she was unsure of him. She had shown no sign of dropping her act. His face lightened. It was all very titillating. He would go along with the deception. Add spice to the courtship.

'Don't do that,' he said. 'Lot of old fuddy-duddies. Wait till you've an evening off and let me know.'

Mary had been warned at home and at the hotel to avoid any relationships with the male guests. They would have only One Thing in mind. But she did so want to go to Astley's, and with a real-life lord. It was all too much to turn down.

'This Friday,' she said cautiously, 'I could maybe say I had to visit my mother in Shoreditch.'

'Shoreditch,' echoed Lord Bewley, appreciating what he heard as her further inventions.

'I could meet you at this side of Westminster Bridge.'

'Seven o'clock,' said Lord Bewley eagerly.

'Seven o'clock,' she murmured and suddenly

flashed a look at him from those blue, blue eyes, eyes which had learned at an early age how to devastate the youths of Shoreditch.

She went quietly out and Lord Bewley fell back on the pillows, gasping. What a jewel! What a charmer!

Still, it all went to show that a girl who had bottom enough to run away from that greedy, debt-ridden father of hers was up to everything and anything. The main thing now was to stop Sir Randolph from interfering in any way. He did not know where his daughter was, and despite a letter from Frederica and a letter from Lord Bewley assuring Sir Randolph of her well-being, he might yet crack and call in the Runners.

So Lord Bewley climbed down from the high bed and went to the writing-table. He penned a letter to Sir Randolph to say that he had discovered Frederica was not indifferent to him and that, provided Sir Randolph did not try to interfere in any way, he, Lord Bewley, would forget about all debts owing.

He signed the letter with a flourish, sanded it and sealed it, and then rang the bell for the footman to take it to the post.

*   *   *

Captain Peter Manners should have been getting ready to go out to call on his mother and fiancée. But he had found excuse after

57

excuse to go down to the office at the back of the hall, always hoping to see that beautiful girl again, but she was nowhere in sight. He did not feel any disloyalty to Belinda Devenham, for he had convinced himself that he had only to *talk* to Frederica again for his intense interest in the girl to go away.

His mother would be furious if he did not call. So, after changing into his best clothes he left his room, smiling at the pretty chambermaid who was strolling along the corridor. She gave him a warm smile in return and he reflected that if she went around smiling at gentlemen guests like that, she might find herself in trouble.

He strode down to the hall.

And there was Frederica in a mob-cap, apron, and print gown crossing the hall.

He was so taken aback at the sight of her that she would have disappeared through the door at the back of the hall had he not suddenly leaped into action.

'Miss Frederica!' he called.

Frederica swung round, miserably aware of her servant's clothes.

He swept her a bow. 'We meet again,' he said.

She had rehearsed all sorts of pretty speeches in her mind for just this moment, but all at once could find nothing to say.

Despite the servant's clothes, he reflected that she was still the most beautiful creature he
58

had ever seen. 'Where do you work?' he asked.

'In the kitchens,' said Frederica miserably, knowing that in the servants' hierarchy, this was the lowest of the low.

'An unhealthy job,' he said quietly, wondering what on earth his mother would think could she see him in such company. 'You do not speak like a servant, nor look like one,' he said.

'Good morning, Lord Bewley,' came Sir Philip's voice from the hall behind them. Frederica's eyes widened in fright, and with a muttered 'Good day,' she turned and fled.

Lord Bewley had seen Frederica, but his eyes had passed over her, eyes which were still full of the beauty of Mary Jones.

CHAPTER FOUR

Poverty is no disgrace to a man, but it is confoundedly inconvenient.
— THE REVEREND SYDNEY SMITH

Mr. Jason Davy seemed immune to the jeering remarks of Sir Philip that he did not seem to show any signs of beginning his debt-collecting.

But Mr. Davy was quietly making his own preparations. He collected some handsome visiting cards with the name 'The Comte de

Versailles' printed in curly letters on them. He had no intention of presenting himself at Lord Braby's house as a common dun. He knew he would have the door slammed in his face by the butler. He still had the fine clothes Colonel Sandhurst had bought for him when he was playing the part of a gentleman. He was glad he had carefully preserved them. He put them on and admired himself in the glass.

He had rented a fine carriage, saying to Colonel Sandhurst that he would claim money for his expenses only if he were successful.

He made his way out to the rented carriage and the rented coachman. 'Grosvenor Square,' he said, 'Lord Braby.' Then he leaned against the squabs and tried to put the ordeal to come out of his mind.

It was a dismal day, with a greasy rain falling. The ragged crossing-sweepers shuffled back and forward through the mud. It was, reflected Mr. Davy wryly, a suitable day for such a dismal business as debt-collecting. It seemed to him that he arrived in Grosvenor Square all too soon. He braced himself. He felt just as he did when he was about to walk on-stage.

Jack, the footman, was on the backstrap. Mr. Davy handed Jack his card. 'Announce me,' he said with a grin, 'and be suitably pompous about it.'

The footman scanned the card and then ran

lightly up the steps and performed a tattoo on the door-knocker.

He handed Mr. Davy's card to the butler and said loudly, 'The Comte de Ver*sales* to see his lordship.'

The butler drew back and held wide the door and Mr. Davy strolled arrogantly up the steps, with a haughty sneer on his face. The butler bowed low. 'I will see if his lordship is at home,' he said.

'Be quick about it, my good man,' Mr. Davy said in a slightly accented drawl. 'I have an engagement with His Royal Highness at noon.'

He was led with great ceremony into a saloon on the ground floor and served with wine and cakes. Mr. Davy looked around him with a practised eye. No shortage of money here, he thought cynically. The carpets were of the finest, as were the ornaments and furniture.

Despite his remark to the butler about his fictitious appointment with the Prince Regent and his high-sounding false name, he expected to be kept waiting, but to his surprise, only five minutes after the wine and cakes had been brought in, Lord Braby himself appeared.

He was a thickset, powerful man wrapped in a banyan of gold cloth and with a turban on his shaven head. After the courtesies had been exchanged, Lord Braby sat down and said, 'And to what do we owe the honour of this visit, Monsieur Le Comte?'

'It is a delicate matter,' said Mr. Davy

haughtily. 'I am close to the Prince Regent and must protect his interests, whether I approve of those interests or not. May I rely on your discretion?'

'Of course, of course,' said Lord Braby expansively.

'It has come to my attention,' said Mr. Davy, studying his fingernails, 'that my royal friend has a new romantic interest.'

'Indeed?'

'You may have heard that my royal patron has a weakness for ladies of mature years.'

'I think everyone has heard that.' Lord Braby's rather piggy eyes gleamed with amusement. 'Who's the latest, hey?'

'It is a certain Lady Fortescue.'

'What! That old harridan who is running that hotel in Bond Street? She must be nearly a hundred!'

'You must see now how it is that discretion is paramount.'

Lord Braby shook his heavy head. 'If the print-shops ever got hold of this one,' he said brutally, 'then Prinny's going to be even more of a laughing-stock than he is already.'

'Nonetheless, that is his latest affection, and I was present with him at the hotel when I heard this Lady Fortescue complaining about unsettled bills.'

'The vulgarity of it!' cried Lord Braby, but he shifted uneasily in his seat.

'Of course, of course. But such creatures as

Lady Fortescue, who forget their standing in life and sink to trade develop a certain ... coarseness.'

Lord Braby began to sweat lightly. His formidable wife wanted an invitation to Clarence House. He, Lord Braby, had just sent a very expensive snuff-box to the Prince Regent to elicit just such an invitation. What if His Erratic Majesty sent it back and told him to settle his bills?

'Look here,' he said with an ingratiating smile. 'Demned if you haven't just reminded me that I myself have an outstanding bill for the Poor Relation. You know how it is. Nothing but bills, bills, bills, and my man of business can be very lax. Tell you what I'll do. I'll send a servant round now with a cheque.'

'I am going that way myself,' said Mr. Davy. 'I would normally consider such a task far beneath me, but anything for Prinny.' He sighed with affected languor.

'I'll see if I can find that demned bill,' said Lord Braby eagerly, and left the room. Mr. Davy smiled to himself. He was sure Lord Braby knew exactly where that bill was and how much it was. He was a not uncommon member of the aristocracy in that he took pleasure in paying out as little money as possible except for his own immediate gratification.

Sure enough, Lord Braby returned after only a short time, brandishing a cheque which

Mr. Davy restrained himself with an effort from looking at.

Mr. Davy then set himself to finish his performance by regaling Lord Braby with several amusing, highly fictitious, and highly scurrilous tales about the Prince Regent before taking his leave.

Later that day, by sheer coincidence, Lord Braby received an invitation to a supper at Clarence House for the Prince Regent. All his regrets at having given that Frenchman money for the bill evaporated.

*　　*　　*

Captain Manners returned to his small and, in his opinion, highly overpriced room at the Poor Relation that evening in a bad temper. He had spent a long and boring day with his beloved and he felt it would not have been boring at all if he could have stopped thinking about one common little scullery maid with the face of an angel.

He decided to go out again to his club and solace himself in purely masculine company. As he reached the landing and was prepared to descend the stairs, something made him turn round and look up. He saw the slim figure of Frederica, no longer in servant's dress but in an expensive muslin gown, looking down at him. The minute she saw him, she coloured and then ran on up the stairs.

All thoughts of masculine company went right out of his head. He turned and began to ascend the staircase.

*   *   *

Sir Philip Sommerville was in a waspish temper as Mr. Davy, urged by the others, once more performed the part of the Comte de Versailles. He thought of all the times when he had bravely and quietly and *modestly* gone about collecting debts, and had *he* ever received such accolades as this popinjay? And that hen-brained fool, Letitia Tonks, was hanging on the mountebank's every word. And there was something wrong.

A consummate liar himself, Sir Philip had a finely tuned ear for the lies of others. The story had started well enough, about how the 'comte' had claimed to be a friend of the Prince Regent, but from then on, the bit about how the prince had taken an interest in the running of the hotel because of its superb food held a hollow note. What had this actor said, really said? Sir Philip became determined to find out. He began to relax. He would wait and bide his time.

'Why did you masquerade as a Frenchman?' asked Lady Fortescue.

'Because it is hard to masquerade as a British peer. Braby would know every name in the country. Also, it's a hanging offence ...

impersonating an English peer. Besides, my supposed friendship with the Prince Regent covered me with respectability.' Mr. Davy saw Sir Philip's pale and calculating eyes resting on him and added hurriedly, 'Enough of my exploits. Let's have a song!'

But Lady Fortescue's still sharp hearing had heard a furtive noise outside the door. 'Someone's listening,' she said sharply. 'Someone's outside the door!'

Mr. Davy darted to the door and swung it wide.

Captain Peter Manners stood staring at them and they all stared back. Then he saw Frederica sitting on a sofa next to Miss Tonks, the candle-light on her golden hair. He bowed and said, 'My apologies. I appear to have wandered into the wrong part of the hotel.'

It was an age when beauty in men was highly appreciated. And there was no denying that this captain was beautiful, with blue-black curls on his proud head, broad shoulders, a trim waist, slim hips, and—Miss Tonks stole a shy look—superb legs. The one flaw in his appearance was in his feet which, although narrow, were of an ordinary size when, for true masculine beauty, he should have had tiny feet.

'Now that you are here, sir,' said Colonel Sandhurst expansively, 'perhaps you would care to join us for a glass of wine.'

'Delighted,' he said promptly.

'We have met in a business capacity but I will

introduce you formally all round,' said the colonel. 'Ladies first. Lady Fortescue, Captain Manners; Captain Manners, Lady Fortescue.' He then introduced Miss Tonks and then came to Frederica. The colonel hesitated. 'And Miss...'

'Black,' said Frederica, rising to her feet and dropping a curtsy. 'Captain Manners and I have met before.'

'Indeed! Where?' demanded Lady Fortescue sharply.

'We collided in the street,' said Frederica. 'Captain Manners knows I am employed here as a scullery maid.'

'Not quite, my dear,' said the colonel. 'Miss Frederica is the daughter of an acquaintance of ours who has volunteered to help in the hotel although she has no reason to.'

The captain's long lashes veiled his expression. So that might explain the expensive gown the girl was wearing and her beautiful voice and manners. The colonel then introduced the men. The captain looked around for somewhere to sit. 'Come sit by me,' said Miss Tonks, and so the captain sat between Miss Tonks and Frederica on the sofa.

Although the captain was as used to London society as he was to army life and knew how to school his expression into a well-bred blank, his thoughts were working furiously behind his polite, bland expression. Everyone knew these hoteliers were aristocrats, with the possible

67

exception of that fellow Davy, who, although grandly dressed in Weston's tailoring, did not have the correct manners of a gentleman. There was too much animation in his face and he moved like an actor impersonating a gentleman. The captain was very rich and had from an early age been used to cutting people who might encroach on him. It was not snobbery but a necessary social art in an era when everyone tried to get money out of everyone else, from the ragged beggars in the streets to the impoverished Irish peers and the ranks of adventurers of both sexes who used every trick and wile they knew to prey on their victims. That was why the marriage to Belinda had been considered so suitable. She was extremely rich as well.

Mr. Davy began to sing, accompanied on the piano by Sir Philip, who had decided to be amiable because he felt sure that Mr. Davy had lied, and exposing the actor and getting rid of him was now only a matter of days.

The captain listened appreciatively to the mellow tones of Mr. Davy's voice singing a humorous ballad. This was much more fun than going to the club or sitting listening to the boring prattle of his fiancée. He tried to erase the latter thought from his shocked mind, but it would not go away. Belinda *was* a bore. And yet, who was to say that this girl next to him—so close that her leg was only inches from his own—would prove to be anything better?

What kind of gently bred female sank to the level of the hotel kitchens? He flicked a glance at her. Her eyes were dancing as she listened to the song. He could smell the light flower perfume she wore. Her hair, no longer hidden by that dreadful mob-cap, gleamed in the light, a stray tendril lying against her cheek.

And then Mr. Davy began to sing a love song full of lost hopes and yearning. The proximity of Frederica, combined with the beauty of the words and the voice which sang them, stirred the captain's very soul. He had an impulse to reach out and take Frederica's hand in his own and restrained himself with an effort. When the singing was over he would have an opportunity to talk to her and perhaps find that under all that beauty lay a dull and stupid mind.

But when Mr. Davy finished his song and sat down to applause, it was Miss Tonks who promptly engaged the captain's attention. Her motives were to protect Frederica from discovery. He answered her questions about his army life and then, to his horror, heard Miss Tonks say in a clear voice, 'I read the social columns and remember reading of your engagement, Captain Manners. My congratulations.'

'Thank you,' he said bleakly, all too aware that Frederica had risen and crossed to the table in the centre of the room where Betty, Lady Fortescue's old servant, had just placed

69

the tea-tray.

Then his attention was caught by the colonel, who was eager for any news of the army. He talked on, all the time aware of Frederica. She was laughing at something Mr. Davy, who had joined her, was saying, her face alight. Who was this Mr. Davy? And all the while the captain chatted easily, until Lady Fortescue rapped her spoon against her cup for silence.

'We have business to discuss, Captain Manners, so perhaps you would care to retire?'

Any gentleman most certainly would, but Captain Manners thought afterwards that he must have become infected by the free and easy ways of these hoteliers because he said easily, 'Unless it is very secret, I would like to stay. I am enjoying the company.'

Frederica resumed her seat. Once more she was next to him but he could sense a certain withdrawal from him. The news of his engagement had hit Frederica with all the force of a bucket of ice-water being dashed in her face. She felt small and silly to have indulged in such romantic dreams about this handsome captain. Once more London seemed a strange and alien place.

'Ahem,' said Lady Fortescue, 'we, that is the Poor Relation, have been asked to do the catering for the Duchess of Darver's party in a week's time.'

'A week!' exclaimed Sir Philip. 'No one gives

us a mere week.'

'Her Grace had already made arrangements to employ Gunter's, but then was told that *we* were more fashionable. Despard and Rossignole, our excellent chefs, say that they can cope provided we find a temporary chef to cope with the dinner here on that evening.'

'Can't find a chef at such short notice,' grumbled Sir Philip. 'Has to be a special chef.'

'Most of our guests will be going to the duchess's party, in any case,' pointed out Lady Fortescue. 'Someone quite ordinary will suffice for that evening.'

'I myself will be going,' put in Captain Manners.

'I have learned quite a bit about the preparation of sauces,' said Frederica. 'Perhaps I could be of help.'

'Oh, but you must come with us to the duchess's,' said Miss Tonks eagerly. 'It is such fun on these occasions. We do not dress as servants. We dress in our very finest. We have waiters and footmen hired to do the real work, but we are expected to serve a little in person to add a cachet to the proceedings.'

'Out of the question,' said Lady Fortescue. 'Frederica must not be seen in society.'

'As to that,' said the colonel, 'there surely can be no harm in her going. I happen to know Lord Bewley is not going to be present.'

'Oh, why don't we just wash *all* our dirty linen in public,' said Sir Philip acidly, pointing

71

to Captain Manners, who was listening with interest to this interchange.'

'Well, well, we shall see,' said Lady Fortescue hurriedly. 'Captain Manners, much as we have enjoyed the infinite pleasure of your company, I beg to remind you that the hour is late.'

'Of course.' He rose and bowed. The ladies curtsied and he took his leave, a very puzzled man. He wandered thoughtfully back to his room, all thoughts of going to his club forgotten.

Was there some shameful scandal about Frederica that she must not appear in society? He shook his head. There could not possibly be. She looked so young and innocent. And why should Lord Bewley figure in it all? Instead of losing interest in her, the brief meeting had fuelled that initial tug of attraction into an obsession. But he would not yet admit that to himself.

*   *   *

On Friday Captain Manners accompanied his mother, Mrs. Devenham, and Belinda to Vauxhall. He had invited his friend, Jack Warren, to accompany them, for both his mother and Mrs. Devenham were widows and the captain felt the need of some masculine support.

Mrs. Devenham and Belinda had insisted on

attending Vauxhall after the 'vulgar' amusements were over, this being considered fashionable, although it disappointed the captain, who still enjoyed a good fireworks display and thought the amusements of Vauxhall were the only reason for going.

They were seated in a box eating wafers of ham and drinking rack punch, a concoction whose base of strong arrack was considered even by hard drinkers to be potent. Unusually enlivened by the punch, Belinda was glowing, and the captain had to admit she looked very fine. He could only wish her conversation were as enlivening as her appearance. She concentrated on studying the passers-by and criticizing the gowns.

But the captain was forced to admit that perhaps he was too nice in his tastes, for Jack Warren happily joined Belinda in her criticisms. Captain Manners glanced idly around at the other boxes and then focused on a couple who were laughing and drinking. He recognized Lord Bewley, he who, for some reason, must not see Frederica. Lord Bewley was entertaining a buxom wench who was dressed in a cheap gown ornamented with cotton lace. Captain Manners was sure he had seen this female before and then realized with a little shock that she was the chambermaid from the hotel.

Nor did the gross-looking Lord Bewley appear to be setting up a mistress, for although they were companionable together, he was treating her with little marks of deference, standing up to adjust her shawl about her shoulders and carving her slivers of ham himself.

The hoteliers were no doubt gathered in that sitting-room of theirs, thought the captain. It would have been jolly to join them.

'What do you think of lavender gloves?' he realized Belinda was asking him.

'For men or for ladies?'

'For men.'

'I do not have very strong feelings on the matter, Miss Belinda,' replied the captain with that mocking gleam darting in his blue eyes that Belinda could not like. She always felt that the captain was laughing at some secret joke.

'Oh, but I do,' said Jack Warren gallantly. 'I have a pair myself, and to that end I ordered a waistcoat and had it made with some very fine twill I got in Italy which has a thin lavender stripe running through it.'

'Some of the material in Italy is very fine,' said Mrs. Devenham. 'When Mr. Devenham was alive, he brought back some bolts of very good silk. Gold colour shot with bronze. I have a gown of it you simply must see, Mr. Warren.'

Jack flicked open his snuff-box and took a delicate pinch. 'I am all anticipation,' he said.

'I would like to promenade for a little,' said Belinda.

'We shall both go for a little walk, my dear,'

said Mrs. Devenham, patting her hand. 'The night air makes my bones stiff if I sit in one place too long.'

Lady Manners leaned forward. 'Perhaps Mr. Warren would be so good as to escort you. I wish a quiet word with my son.'

Jack went off with a lady on either arm.

'Now, Peter,' said Lady Manners sternly. 'What are you about?'

'I do not understand you, Mama.'

'No? I arranged this engagement for you to Miss Devenham and thereby secured you a beautiful lady with a handsome dowry. And yet there is an indifference in your attitude towards her which displeases me.'

'As you say, you arranged it, Mother. Love did not enter into the equation.'

'Love. Tcha! Why cannot you be more like your friend, Mr. Warren, who is gallantry itself. I also fail to understand why you will not stay in your family home but needs must go to that dreadful Limmer's which is full of Corinthians.'

'I am no longer at Limmer's. I am at the Poor Relation.'

'I know we are very wealthy, but there is no need to throw good money away,' said Lady Manners tartly. She showed no evidence of her son's good looks, or indeed of ever having had them. She was a round woman—round figure, round plump cheeks. 'But as you are there,' she added, 'I know the Devenhams have been longing to have dinner there, for the cooking is renowned.'

He had a sudden vision of Frederica sweating in the kitchens and being told he was entertaining his fiancée abovestairs in the dining-room. But he said aloud, 'I will arrange it for one evening, but they are fully booked and it is very hard—'

'Fiddlesticks! I happen to know that residents have first priority when it comes to inviting parties. I am disappointed in you. Furthermore, you are not making your mark on society.'

'I do not need to make my mark on society,' said the captain with a certain hauteur. 'I am *in* society.'

'But not a leader. You must cultivate some eccentricity. There is a captain in the Guards who has achieved a certain notoriety by engaging to climb around the furniture of a room without once setting foot on the floor.'

'Coxcomb,' commented the captain.

'You are being a trifle *difficile*, my son. Even the cream of society cultivate their little eccentricities. The Marquess of Queensberry once sent a message fifty miles in thirty minutes by having it thrown from hand to hand in a cricket ball. Buck Whalley walked to Jerusalem in a long blue coat, top-boots, and buckskins. Now Lord Harewood's claim to fame is that he imitates the prince in everything—dresses the same, has the same mannerisms; and Lord Petersham is famous for his snuff-boxes, or no one would pay him a bit of attention; and old Lord Dudley speaks exactly what is on his mind. And who is that fellow who walks into every room on his hands?'

She paused to draw breath and the captain said mockingly, 'I am a sad disappointment to you, Mother. In truth, I do not know any fellow who walks into the room on his hands, nor do I care to.'

She put her hand on his and said fondly, 'You are the most handsome man in London, but you lack *style*. Mr. Warren is all charm and gallantry to Belinda and laughs so delightfully at everything she says.'

'That could be because she does not bore him.'

'What an awful thing to say.' His mother looked at him in sudden amazement. 'Never say you are looking for an *intelligent* female!'

'God forbid,' he said lightly, but the irony in his voice was lost on his mother, who looked relieved. 'Here comes Belinda. Do try to be a little more charming.'

And so the captain adjusted his shirt frills, braced himself and set out to be pleasant to Belinda, and almost succeeded in banishing Frederica's pretty face from his mind.

*   *   *

Lord Bewley felt at peace with the world as he strolled under the trees with Mary. He had called her Frederica and she had exclaimed in surprise that her name was Mary Jones and he had grinned to himself and decided to go along with what he thought of as an amusing masquerade. He had enjoyed the evening earlier in Astley's, relishing his companion's naïve delight in every spectacle. Had Lord Bewley not been convinced he was walking with a young lady of good background, he would have dragged her into the bushes and had her skirts over her head in no time at all, and so it was as well for Mary that he did not know that she really was a chambermaid. Mary was thinking that it all went to show that all the lectures she had received at home and in the hotel on the vicious, licentious manners of gentlemen towards their underlings was not true. Why, Lord Bewley treated her like a real lady!

*   *   *

Earlier that evening, Lady Fortescue was aware of a strange atmosphere when she entered the dining-room on the arm of Colonel Sandhurst. She, the colonel, and Sir Philip served the first course before letting the waiters take over. It had been one of the main attractions of the hotel before Despard's superb cooking became the main item. Every table was full. But it was not that. It was the way all eyes turned avidly in her direction when she entered, the way heads bent towards each other and excited whispering arose.

'Dear me,' she said loudly to the colonel while her black eyes raked the room, 'do I have a smut on my nose or is my gown undone?'

'Nothing like that,' said the colonel mildly.

The whispering withered and died under Lady Fortescue's haughty glare. But like bad children, the diners would occasionally steal sly glances at her and then giggle.

Lady Fortescue summoned Sir Philip. 'Someone has been spreading scurrilous gossip about me. I *smell* it. Find out what it is and scotch it!'

'Gladly,' said Sir Philip. He saw young Fetter, a Bond Street lounger if ever there was one, sitting with a party by the window. Fetter, he knew, went to Limmer's after dinner and could be found in the coffee room. Sir Philip decided to follow him there and winkle any gossip out of him.

CHAPTER FIVE

I used to get my sulphur-coloured gloves from the Palais Royal. When the war broke out in '93 I was cut off from them for nine years. Had it not been for a lugger which I specially hired to smuggle them, I might have been reduced to English tan.

—Sir Arthur Conan Doyle

Miss Tonks and Frederica were alone in the sitting-room the following evening. Dinner was in progress in the hotel dining-room downstairs and the others would not join them until it was over. Mr. Davy had gone off to see some actor friends, or rather, Miss Tonks hoped they were actor friends and not actress friends.

Both were hemming handkerchiefs. 'Captain Manners is very handsome, is he not?' said Miss Tonks, biting off a thread with her rather rabbity teeth.

'Yes,' said Frederica bleakly. Now that she no longer had the captain to dream about—for how could one dream about a man who was engaged to another?—she felt increasingly uneasy about her situation. What was to become of her? The only future for any gently bred girl was marriage. She could beg the hoteliers to let her stay with them, but in doing so she would dash all hopes of marriage. It had been forcibly borne in on her the last time she had seen the captain that no man of the ton was going to stoop to marry a girl who had so far forgotten her position in life as to work in the kitchens of a Bond Street hotel.

'It is a pity he is engaged,' pursued Miss Tonks, 'for I feel he would have made an ideal partner for you.'

'I have put myself beyond the pale by working here,' said Frederica. 'Not that I am ungrateful to you all, for I would rather do anything than be forced to marry Lord Bewley. I saw him. He is even worse than I imagined.'

'As to that,' said Miss Tonks, 'our first cook, Harriet James, became the Duchess of Rowcester.'

Frederica begged to hear more and Miss Tonks regaled her with stories to prove that in some odd way working at the hotel had meant a grand marriage for her old friend rather than social disgrace. But Frederica, who had not been *out* and therefore did not know any social gossip, listened indulgently, and thought the spinster was telling fairy stories. Grand gentlemen did not risk social censure. She had learned that much on the hunting field. She remembered hearing of a lord who had married his cook. She was allowed to be a good cook, but the men had said it was a pity because naturally one could no longer invite this lord anywhere and so he had seen the sufficient folly of his ways and removed his unfashionable spouse to Italy, to a place where there was only the British consul and his wife to snub them instead of the whole of English society.

'If you do not want to go with us to the duchess's,' said Miss Tonks, disappointed that her stories had not seemed to bring any sparkle back to Frederica's eyes, 'that is perfectly in order. But it will be such fun. Lady Fortescue suggests we call on Madame Verné tomorrow to purchase a ball gown for you. It is very short notice, but sometimes they have one that has been ordered but find that the lady has gone abroad. Perhaps you feel it might ruin your chances socially when you make your come-out at the Season.'

'As far as I know,' said Frederica, carefully smoothing the handkerchief she was hemming on her knee, 'I am not to have a come-out. Should I return home, I would still be forced into marriage with either Lord Bewley, or some other man.'

Miss Tonks was about to say that Lord Bewley had no intention now of marrying her but remembered in time that Frederica knew nothing about that ransom or that any of them had discussed her with Lord Bewley, and so said brightly, 'Then, in that case, do say you will come to the dressmaker with me tomorrow.'

Frederica's eyes held a flicker of amusement. 'I thought one did not go to the shopkeeper but that the shopkeeper came to one's home.'

'True, very true,' said Miss Tonks seriously. 'But I am become quite *sharp* in the ways of business and can *haggle* the better when I am on the premises. Ah, I hear the others.'

Frederica felt a little tug at her heart as she looked towards the door. She thought she had put the captain out of her mind, and yet, it would somehow be wonderful if he walked in again to join them. But Sir Philip was first through the door and looking very triumphant. Shortly afterwards, he was followed by Colonel Sandhurst and Lady Fortescue.

Betty and John, Lady Fortescue's old servants, came in bearing the tea-tray. 'Those cakes are mine,' cried Frederica. 'I am advancing into pastry.'

Shrugging off a mental picture of a pretty Frederica wading through a giant bowl of dough, Sir Philip said, 'I have news of our Mr. Davy which will shock you all!'

'Now what?' asked Miss Tonks acidly. 'You've always had your knife into that man, and do you know why? You're jealous because he managed to get that money out of Lord Braby, and with no trouble at all!'

Sir Philip waved his hands, looking in that moment to Frederica like some elderly monkey, for the palms of his hands were stained with cochineal, a fashion which had recently been exploded but which Sir Philip still favoured from time to time.

'Just wait till you hear this,' he crowed. 'Our famous Mr. Davy pretended to be a certain Comte de Versailles.'

'We know that,' growled the colonel, 'and very clever it was, too.'

'What you don't know'—Sir Philip's pale

eyes fastened on Lady Fortescue—'is that Mr. Davy told Lord Braby that his aristocratic interest in unpaid debts owing to the Poor Relation rose from the fact that his oh-so-dear friend, the Prince of Wales, was spoony about Lady Fortescue here.'

There was a shocked silence.

'Nonsense,' said the colonel finally.

'True,' cackled Sir Philip, enjoying the consternation on their faces. 'And this is the fellow you are all so keen to have join us.'

'There must be some mistake.' Miss Tonks looked pleadingly at the others.

'I do not think so,' said Lady Fortescue slowly. 'That explains why we have had so many from court circles at our tables and, yes, it also explains why everyone has been paying so promptly. In fact, Lady Tarrant had not paid her hotel bill and yet she sent the money round this afternoon.' Lady Fortescue began to laugh, her black eyes sparkling, and Frederica, looking at her, realized that Lady Fortescue must have been handsome in her youth, for under the wrinkles and paint lay the shadow of lost beauty. 'How splendid!' Lady Fortescue cried. 'How delightful to be made to feel so *wicked* at my great age. I am much indebted to Mr. Davy.'

'Have you no care for your reputation?' cried the colonel. 'I'll horsewhip that mountebank!'

Lady Fortescue continued to laugh, a

84

surprisingly girlish laugh. 'Oh, don't you see,' she said finally, 'it is all so ridiculous that society will come to its senses, particularly when they find out that this comte does not exist and realize Lord Braby has been gulled. Everyone will laugh at him, which he richly deserves, and will admire us the more.'

'You mean you are going to let him get away with this?' Sir Philip could hardly believe his ears.

'I shall speak to Mr. Davy quite severely, of course.' Lady Fortescue threw a flirtatious look at the colonel. 'Do not look such daggers, my dear. A storm in a teacup. A nothing. A trivial bit of gossip which has lasted long enough to get the bills paid.'

'Well, as there are no longer any outstanding bills,' said Sir Philip waspishly, 'what's the point of giving this poxy actor bed and board?'

'He is just as important to the hotel as any of us,' said Miss Tonks hotly.

'Why?' Sir Philip stared contemptuously at her. 'The cachet of this hotel is because we're top ton. What's the cachet in having an actor waiting table? There's enough of them doing that already, yes, and at every chop-house in London, too.'

'You're jealous,' said Miss Tonks. 'Yes, jealous. Because he's younger than you and just as clever.'

'Let us not squabble,' said Lady Fortescue. 'I shall reprimand Mr. Davy myself as the

85

matter concerns me. Mr. Davy is still on trial. Agreed?'

'As far as I am concerned, he is finished,' shouted Sir Philip and stormed out of the room.

The colonel cleared his throat. 'I can well understand his wrath. To sully your name in such a way, dear lady...'

'If I thought for a moment any of that ridiculous gossip would stick, I should be very upset,' said Lady Fortescue mildly. 'But by tomorrow night, if I am again faced with bent heads, whispers, and avid looks in the dining-room, I shall be very much surprised!'

*   *   *

Sir Philip went along to Limmer's and sulked in the coffee room for almost two hours. At last he left, but instead of returning to the hotel he walked along that narrow bit called the Bond Street Straits, rather unsteadily, as he had drunk two bottles of wine. It was when he turned aimlessly into Stafford Street, which was lit only by one flickering parish lamp that, too late, he became aware of danger. It was the way the man was approaching him, a dark figure, black against the surrounding gloom, that warned him. He could see the head turning this way and that, making sure there were no witnesses. Sir Philip felt for his sword-stick and realized with dismay that he had left it behind.

The man, seeing there was no one else in the street but himself and Sir Philip, advanced holding a long, wicked-looking knife. 'Hand over your money,' he said in a hoarse whisper, 'or it will be the worse for you.'

Sir Philip felt quite faint. He had been given the day's takings from the guests, the dining-room, and the coffee room by the colonel, and he had forgotten to lock it all in the safe. He had discovered the money still on him when he had paid his shot at Limmer's.

'I haven't any money,' he said feebly.

The man seized him by the cravat with the hand that was not holding the knife. 'You old varmint,' he said. 'Give it 'ere.'

The moon high above pitiless London slipped out from behind a cloud. The man was shaking Sir Philip as a dog shakes a rat and he could feel his senses going. And then suddenly there was a loud *thwack*. Sir Philip, his cravat suddenly freed, lurched and swayed, and then felt himself caught and held by a strong arm. He thought he was being attacked again and choked out a 'help' which sounded like a bleat.

'Steady, Sommerville,' said a voice in his ear. 'It is I, Davy.'

Gasping, Sir Philip twisted himself away from that arm. His assailant lay stretched on the ground and Mr. Davy was holding a stout cudgel.

When he recovered his wits and stood there while Mr. Davy shouted at the top of his voice for the watch, Sir Philip's first feeling was one of pure rage that this actor, whom he had hoped to get rid of, should have rescued him. The rattle of the watch sounded at the end of the street and soon the watch himself, followed by the parish constable, came up to hear Mr. Davy's report. The assailant had recovered consciousness and was dragged off.

Sir Philip managed to choke out his thanks. 'Let's go to Limmer's and have some gin punch to sustain us,' said Mr. Davy. 'But you have not told me yet what you were doing wandering about the streets at this hour on your own.'

'Thinking,' said Sir Philip curtly. 'Tell you about it when we sit down.'

They made their way silently back to Limmer's, Sir Philip still staggering slightly but refusing help from Mr. Davy. It was when they were seated over a bottle of wine and Mr. Davy looked expectantly at Sir Philip, that Sir Philip decided to get even with Miss Tonks. For was it not the besotted Miss Tonks who was responsible for introducing this lower-class body into their exclusive hotel? Besides, Sir Philip had marked Miss Tonks down as his own. Not for love, not for any sexual reasons— Heaven forbid!—but because he was an old man and would need someone to look after his comforts when he retired. He would need someone to run his house and deal with the servants and wait on him hand and foot. Miss

Tonks would have been only too pleased to promise to do all of that in exchange for the coveted title of 'Lady' only a short time ago, a time before she had ever heard of Jason Davy.

'I was walking because I was upset and worried,' said Sir Philip.

'Anything wrong at the hotel?'

'Not that. It is Miss Tonks.'

'Letitia? She is not ill, is she?'

His familiar use of Miss Tonks's first name hardened Sir Philip's resolve. The hissing sounds from behind him, where a group of Corinthians were spitting into the fire, passing the late hour in a spitting competition accompanied by loud beefy laughs, jangled Sir Philip's nerves, and he ignored the voice of conscience in his head, which was screaming at him that he was about to make a cake of himself.

'You have taken her affections away from me,' said Sir Philip.

Mr. Davy looked at the elderly gentleman facing him and thought uncharitably that Sir Philip looked exactly in that moment like an evil old tortoise. But he fought down his feeling of repugnance and said quietly, 'Go on.'

'We are all old and cannot go on in this hotel business forever,' said Sir Philip. 'Naturally, as you are not one of us, you do not know of our plans for the future. Colonel Sandhurst and Lady Fortescue plan to marry and retire to the country.' Again that pang of conscience, for was not he himself attracted to Lady Fortescue? But Miss Tonks deserved to be taught a lesson. 'Miss Tonks and I have a certain understanding that we too will join forces and spend our declining years together.'

There was a long silence and then Mr. Davy said, 'Miss Tonks is considerably younger than you, sir.'

'Oh, she's a lot older than she looks,' said Sir Philip, maliciously hammering another nail into Miss Tonks's coffin.

'I have not done anything to take Miss Tonks's affections away from you,' said Mr. Davy firmly. 'Miss Tonks and I are good friends, that is all.'

'But you're taking them away by *being* with us,' howled Sir Philip. The spitting behind him stopped. He turned round and said waspishly, 'Oh, pray do not let me keep you from your intellectual amusements,' and the spitting started again.

'You wish me to leave?' asked Mr. Davy. Sir Philip studied him but the actor's face registered nothing stronger than polite interest.

'Only for the sake of Miss Tonks's well-being and to bring happiness to an old man.' Sir Philip took out a large handkerchief and dabbed his dry eyes. 'Besides, that lie you told about Lady Fortescue being Prinny's paramour did not go down very well.'

'How did she find out?'

'Someone felt it their duty to tell her,' said Sir Philip piously.

That someone being you, thought Mr. Davy.

'Is Lady Fortescue very angry?' he asked.

'Very,' said Sir Philip with relish. 'It would be better for your dignity for you to leave quietly before you are ordered to leave.'

'Perhaps you are right.' Mr. Davy poured them both another glass of wine. 'How are you feeling now after your adventure?'

'Tolerable,' said Sir Philip. 'Thank'ee,' he added gruffly. He remembered the money still reposing in a bag in one of his capacious pockets and tossed back his wine with one gulp. 'Had better go. Do you come, too?'

'I will stay here for a while. The Poor Relation is only a step away. I doubt if anyone will attack you in the middle of Bond Street.'

By the time Sir Philip climbed into bed he had talked his conscience down. It was all for the best. They had all lowered themselves enough in life by engaging in trade. Miss Tonks should be spared becoming involved with a man well beneath her in social station.

*　　　*　　　*

Sir Philip, exhausted by his adventure and the amount he had drunk, slept late into the following afternoon. Unfortunately for him, Mr. Davy did not. Nor was it in Mr. Davy's

91

nature to slink away.

He first of all sought an audience with Lady Fortescue. She inclined her head as she listened to his apology and then said, 'Do not do such a thing again, Mr. Davy. If you are to collect debts for this hotel, then you must go about it in a less convoluted way. As it so happens, your fiction frightened the rest of our debtors into paying. But there is much to do here. We are often plagued with Bond Street loungers in the coffee room and the waiters are unable to cope with them. Until we decide what to do with you, we will put you in charge of the coffee room.'

'Am I expected to wear livery?' asked Mr. Davy.

'No, you are expected to dress in your finest and look and behave like one of us. People come to this hotel to be served by us who are often in many respects their betters.' This last was said without a trace of humour.

'I will go about my duties,' he said, 'but first I would like to speak to Miss Tonks about something.'

'She and Frederica are next door. A rather plain ball gown was purchased for Frederica, and they are both set on embellishing it. They are probably using the sitting-room.'

The apartment next door had a small sitting-room, not much used because they all preferred to use the one in the hotel, but it was there that Mr. Davy found Miss Tonks alone, studying fashion-plates, her work-basket open beside her.

'Where is Miss Frederica?' he asked.

'In the kitchens. She has but left. Did you want to speak to her?'

'No. To you.'

Miss Tonks looked at him as shyly as a young girl. 'I am at your service, sir.'

'Have you seen Sir Philip today?'

'No, but the snores coming from his room are quite dreadful.'

'I met Sir Philip by chance last night. I rescued him from a footpad in Stratford Street.'

Miss Tonks clasped her hands, her eyes shining. 'How very brave of you, sir. Pray, tell me all about it.'

'Later, perhaps. But what happened was this. Sir Philip and I repaired to Limmer's and Sir Philip said it would be better for you if I left the hotel.'

'For *me*? Why on earth? I was the one who brought you here.'

'Sir Philip is understandably jealous of me. He has some mad idea that you might transfer your affections from him to me.'

'But ... b-but ... b-b-but ...,' stammered poor Miss Tonks, 'Sir Philip has no hold on my affections. No, that is not true. I am fond of Sir Philip despite his waspish ways, as I am fond of Lady Fortescue and Colonel Sandhurst. That is all. I will be honest with you. There was a time after my friend, Mrs. Budley, was married that I felt alone in the world. Working here, I have become used to company, and I dread being alone again. On the road home from the wedding in Warwickshire, Sir Philip was very friendly and companionable. I began to think that when Lady Fortescue and the colonel retired and set up house together, perhaps I could marry Sir Philip, not for any reason other than not to be left alone. But on our return Sir Philip fell in love with that common gross woman, Mrs. Budge, whom you were hired first of all to dislodge. I realized I could never tolerate Sir Philip as a husband.' She flushed delicately. 'With Mrs. Budge, he betrayed certain coarse appetites which I ... oh, dear me, this is *so* embarrassing ... I had expected would have disappeared with age. Ahem.' Poor Miss Tonks shuffled her narrow feet and looked miserable. 'What I am trying to say, Mr. Davy, is that there is no reason to leave on my behalf, and furthermore'—she gave a little gulp—'I value our friendship.'

'Then let it continue,' he said gaily. 'I have been put in charge of the coffee room and must go about my duties.' He bowed and kissed the back of her hand, smiled at her and left.

Miss Tonks sat for a long time with the hand he had just kissed held against her cheek.

* * *

Frederica was alone in the kitchens. Despard, his assistant, and the rest of the kitchen staff had gone down to Oxford Street to watch the guards marching past. She was beating white of egg to make meringues and wondering if the mixture would ever become stiff enough. She was enjoying her work, however, not quite realizing that the two doting chefs made sure she never did anything too strenuous.

She heard footsteps coming down the narrow area steps outside and then heard a knock at the door. She went to answer it, expecting to open the door to a tradesman, but found herself staring up into the handsome face of Captain Manners. He was clutching a bunch of flowers.

'For you,' he said, holding them out.

Frederica took the flowers and dropped a curtsy. 'How very kind of you, sir,' she said. 'Would you care to step inside? I can give you a glass of wine ... or tea ... or something.'

He followed her in. She poured him a glass of wine from a bottle which Despard had opened earlier. 'I shall go on with my work,' said Frederica, 'for the others will be back presently. They are gone to watch the guards parade along Oxford Street.'

He sipped his wine and studied her as she beat the meringue mixture. Her face was flushed, for the kitchen was very hot, her nose was shining, damp tendrils of hair were escaping from under the mob-cap she wore, and he thought she looked prettier than ever.

'Let me do that,' he said, getting up. 'You look as if you need some help.'

Frederica sat down with a little sigh. 'Despard beats eggs like a machine and his whites become stiff in no time at all, but it seems to take me ages.'

He glanced at her small white hands. 'You are a puzzle, Miss Frederica.'

'How so?'

'You have the dress and manners of a lady. Your hands are fine and white and you have never done kitchen work before.'

'How do you know that?'

'Simple. The servants who work in these kitchen basements have complexions like clay and red, work-worn hands.'

Frederica knew she should keep her secret to herself, but even while beating eggs he looked tall and aristocratic. She did not want him to think she was a mere servant.

'If I tell you, sir, will you promise not to betray me?'

'On my heart.'

'My name is really Frederica Gray. I am the only daughter of Sir Randolph and Lady Gray. They ran up a large bill here and did not pay it. Colonel Sandhurst was sent to collect the money. He arrived in our grounds on the night I was running away from home. You see, my father had arranged a marriage for me to Lord Bewley and ... and ... I could not go

96

through with it. Colonel Sandhurst did not collect his debt. He decided instead to offer me shelter here until my father came to his senses.'

'I do not think these hoteliers are very good protectors,' commented the captain. 'Lord Bewley is resident at this hotel and you are condemned to work in the kitchens.'

'As to that, Lord Bewley has never met me and does not know where I am. And I only work a few hours here each day and Monsieur Despard, the chef, is very kind to me. It is,' she added with quaint seriousness, 'very important for a lady to know how to cook.'

'It is very unconventional behaviour,' he said with a touch of severity.

Frederica gave him a candid look. 'Have you considered your own behaviour, Captain Manners? I am grateful for the flowers, but surely a gentleman does not present flowers to a scullery maid unless his intentions are of the worst.'

'Had I believed for a moment you were really a scullery maid ... there, the mixture is perfect ... I would not have dreamt of such a thing. I do not seduce servants.'

'But you are engaged to be married.' She removed her hideous mob-cap and her hair gleamed gold in the dim light from the barred window above her head.

'I am well aware of it. It amused me to find out more about you.'

'Now you have'—Frederica's voice held an

edge—'you may take yourself off, for my companions in labour will soon be here and I must be careful of my reputation.'

For one moment, a sort of baffled anger flashed in his blue eyes, to be replaced by his normal amused and slightly mocking look.

He bowed. 'Your servant, Miss Gray. No doubt we shall not meet again.'

'Now that *would* be correct and conventional,' said Frederica. Her eyes danced and he felt pompous and stuffy.

But when he had left, the laughter died in Frederica's eyes and she sat slowly down at the table again and clutched her cap in her small hands. She felt she had had a brief glimpse of freedom before sinking back into the person she had always been at home, crushed and small and somehow always in the wrong. She should have behaved like any well-bred miss despite her odd circumstances. She had been taught how to simper and flatter. She had even been taught how to laugh by a music teacher. A fashionable laugh was supposed to tinkle melodiously down the scale. He would think her a hurly-burly hoyden.

* * *

Captain Manners met his friend, Mr. Jack Warren, in Bond Street and they walked together towards the Bond Street Straits. Jack was talking lightly of the latest scandal when

98

the captain suddenly said abruptly, 'Dammit, she's *adorable*.'

Jack stopped in mid-sentence and stared at his friend. 'Miss Belinda Devenham?'

Captain Manners collected his wits.

'Who else?' he asked lightly.

CHAPTER SIX

It is seven-and-forty years since I looked upon that circle of dandies, and where, now, are their dainty little hats, their wonderful waistcoats, and their boots in which one could arrange one's cravat? They lived strange lives, these men, and they died strange deaths—some by their own hands, some as beggars, some in a debtor's gaol, some, like the most brilliant of them all, in a madhouse in a foreign land.

—SIR ARTHUR CONAN DOYLE

To Sir Philip's dismay, not only did Mr. Davy appear more entrenched in the hotel life than he had ever been before, but Lady Fortescue had been proved right. He had heard the gossip and it was all against Lord Braby, about how he had been gulled by some false aristocrat into paying his shot at the Poor Relation. Lord Braby himself had arrived in great wrath at the hotel, only to be met by an icy Lady Fortescue who pointed out that he was making an even greater fool of himself by cursing about a debt which he was supposed to have paid anyway. If, she said, some unknown friend had taken it upon himself to trick his lordship into paying up, then he had only himself to blame.

Having dealt with Lord Braby to her satisfaction, Lady Fortescue realized she had almost forgotten about the problem of Mary Jones, the chambermaid. She sent for Miss Tonks and asked if Mary had been getting into trouble with any of the male guests.

'I have kept an eye on her,' said Miss Tonks, 'and to be fair, she is behaving impeccably. Her manner, which appeared a trifle saucy and bold when she came here, has changed and she is modest and well-behaved and, despite her looks, *that* appears enough to quell any advances. I worked with her the other morning. It is amazing how many of our gentlemen do contrive to be awake when she walks into the room, but she goes quickly and quietly about her duties. I thought Lord Bewley was a trifle bold in his remarks to her and he seemed quite angry when I followed her into his room, but she appeared not to notice.'

'You'll have me out of a job,' Mary was whispering to Lord Bewley in the corridor outside his room at that very moment.

'What do you care?' he said with a grin. 'You can always go home.'

'What? To Shoreditch? Back to sharing a

bed with three little sisters?'

'Oh, you're a caution,' said Lord Bewley with relish. 'I don't know how you do it.'

'Do what, my lord?'

'Keep up that act.'

'I ain't acting, my lord.'

'Have it your way, my sweeting. What about coming out with me again? What about the opera? Can't stand it meself, but prepared to make the sacrifice.'

'I would like to see Grimaldi at the Wells,' said Mary.

'Sadler's Wells it is,' said Lord Bewley heartily. He, too, wanted to see the famous clown Grimaldi. He was struck afresh at how close in their interests and pleasures he and this girl were. 'When?'

'Thursday night,' said Mary. 'They're all going to the Duchess of Darver's party and I can slip away.'

'Pick you up outside the old Pantheon building in Oxford Street at seven then,' said Lord Bewley gleefully.

Mary dropped a curtsy and scurried off, well satisfied. She was secretly beginning to entertain hopes of marriage. The sane and sensible part of her mind told her this was quite mad, but the other part dreamt of being 'my lady.' She studied the grand ladies who stayed at the hotel, noticing their speech and manners. She had quickly learned to parry passes made at her by the male guests. She went up to the small room she shared with two other maids and practised walking up and down with a book on her head. Then she talked to herself out loud, trying to refine her vowels. Dreams might just come true if you worked hard enough at them.

*   *   *

Frederica was not looking forward to working at the duchess's party. Captain Manners had said he would be there—but he would be there with his fiancée, entrenched in his own world and miles from hers. If she had not run away from home to this hotel, she would still be a part of that world. But that was silly. If she had stayed at home, she would have had to marry Lord Bewley and she would never even have seen the captain.

Miss Tonks noticed her downcast looks and misinterpreted them. 'You must not think it will be at all shaming,' she said. 'We dress in our very finest and Sir Philip is trying to get jewels for us. Mr. Hamlet is tired of us, but Sir Philip is convinced he can persuade Rundell and Bridge to lend us some jewels for the evening.'

'Why should great jewellers such as Mr. Hamlet and Rundell and Bridge bother to lend us gems?'

'Advertisement. It pays to advertise. We are supposed to murmur discreetly to guests who

102

might admire what we are wearing that they can be purchased at so and so's.'

A fastidious part of Frederica's mind considered this all rather vulgar. But she was consoled with the thought of her gown. It was so very beautiful. It was of blonde satin with an overdress of white lace fastened with gold clasps. The overdress had been Miss Tonks's inspiration, as she had pointed out that both satin and the blonde colour were a trifle old for a girl of Frederica's years who ought to be wearing white muslin.

'Sir Philip is trying to get you a pearl tiara,' said Miss Tonks. 'I am sure he will succeed. Mr. Davy wanted to go, but Sir Philip got very cross and rude and said poor Mr. Davy had not the *standing* in society to impress the jewellers. Mr. Davy is constantly being reminded he is not a gentleman, and yet his manners are faultless compared to those of Sir Philip.'

'Mr. Davy has too much animation, enthusiasm, and kindness in his manner to be a real gentleman,' said Frederica drily.

'Do you think,' said Miss Tonks in a rush, 'that Mr. Davy feels anything for me at all?'

Frederica looked at her in surprise. She had never previously thought of anyone above the age of, say, twenty-five, as having any tender feelings at all. But there was the elderly colonel obviously pining after the equally elderly Lady Fortescue, and so Miss Tonks, who was in her forties, could therefore be expected to still

103

dream of romance.

'I had not really thought of it,' Frederica said cautiously. 'Mr. Davy does appear to respect you.'

'Oh, *respect*,' mourned Miss Tonks, who forgot that in her impoverished days she had craved respect. 'Let us talk about you. Captain Manners will be there.'

Frederica turned pink. 'So I heard him say. But he will no doubt be accompanying his fiancée.'

'He is not yet married.'

'He will be,' said Frederica with an odd look in her eyes. 'In order to end the engagement, she will need to be the one to break it, and ... and I cannot envisage any lady doing that.'

'Oh, is that why I get the impression you are not looking forward to this party?'

Frederica bit her lip and then said in a low voice, 'I am persuaded I do not feel anything for Captain Manners at all. How could I? I barely know him. He called on me.'

'Where?'

'He came down to the kitchens and gave me a bunch of flowers.'

'He had no right to do that. I hope Despard sent him away.'

'There was no one there but me. The rest had gone to watch the military parade in Oxford Street.'

'Oh, dear, I do not like this at all. As far as the captain is concerned, you are a servant. His intentions are suspect.'

Frederica was about to say that Captain Manners knew exactly who she was for she had told him but somehow she could not bring herself to explain that to Miss Tonks.

'I can look after myself,' she said instead. 'I reminded him of his engagement. He will not approach me again. But you seemed to entertain hopes of a romance for me a moment before. Why is it now so impossible?'

'I am a romantic and sometimes very silly. I had forgot your position here and how it must look to someone who does not know your circumstances. Lord Bewley does not know who you are?'

'He has only seen me once and briefly. He showed no interest in me at all.'

'Of course,' went on Miss Tonks, fretting away at the problem, 'the very fact that you are with *us*, that he met you with us in our private sitting-room may very well lead Captain Manners to believe you are of gentle birth. One has only to look at you. Yes, yes, I am persuaded that is it. Never give up hope,' she added sententiously. 'Here I am at my age pining over an out-of-work actor, and yet I refuse to see the folly of my ways.'

Frederica wondered what Captain Manners's fiancée was like. She found herself hoping that she was very plain. She did not rate her own looks very highly. Blonde hair was not fashionable. Perhaps this lady might have red hair or something awful like that. But underneath all these fretting thoughts ran one strong one. Frederica really did not want to go. She was sensible enough to know that to show her face in society meant ruin of any future chances of a decent marriage. She had not really believed Miss Tonks's stories of friends who had married well despite working at the hotel. She only knew that she was seventeen, nearly eighteen, and that it was different for these ancients who ran the hotel. Their life was over, she thought with all the brutality of youth. And yet, charming pictures of her remorse-stricken father welcoming her home and promptly setting about to give her a Season were ridiculous. She gave a little sigh. She had burnt her boats and there was no going back now.

* * *

As was usual before these events, they all met in the sitting-room for a 'dress rehearsal' the evening before, Lady Fortescue insisting they all must look grand.

Frederica, in all the glory of her new gown, began to feel her first flutter of pleasurable excitement. Lady Fortescue was in violet silk, flounced and gored and with a long train. On her white hair she wore a splendid diamond tiara and had a collar of diamonds round her neck. Miss Tonks was in leaf-green silk shot

106

with bronze, a Turkish turban on her head and a ruby necklace at her neck.

The gentlemen were very fine in black evening dress, with knee-breeches and embroidered waistcoats. Mr. Davy was wearing the clothes which the colonel had previously ordered for him from Weston, and Miss Tonks thought mistily that there would not be a finer-looking man at the party.

Jack, the footman, was guarding the chest in which the jewels had arrived. A pretty pearl-and-gold tiara was selected for Frederica and a fine pearl-and-gold necklace. They crowded around her as she put the jewels on, the colonel saying in an odd choked sort of voice which made Lady Fortescue glare at him that Miss Frederica would be the prettiest thing London had ever seen. The colonel's conscience was troubling him sorely. Sooner or later, Frederica would need to return to her home, and once there she would learn that she had been taken under their wing only so that they could recoup the money her father owed them. Miss Tonks felt another sort of pang as she surveyed the dazzling beauty that was Frederica and noticed the open admiration in Mr. Davy's eyes. If only the gods had chosen to invest *her* with beauty. It was all very well to talk of character and worthier traits, but in that moment poor Miss Tonks felt she could have sold her soul to the devil for just one evening of beauty.

Having admired each other sufficiently, they removed their jewellery and handed it back to Jack, who locked it up in the strong-box for safekeeping.

*   *   *

Mary Jones slipped up to the bedchambers, a bunch of keys in her hand. One of the guests, Lady Tonbridge, she knew had gone to the country for a few days, leaving most of her extensive wardrobe behind. Mary was determined to dress like a fine lady for that outing to Sadler's Wells with Lord Bewley.

She jumped guiltily at every noise. She knew her bosses were upstairs in their private sitting-room. Taking a deep breath, she selected the key to Lady Tonbridge's room and slipped inside, locking the door behind her for safety.

Mary went through to the bedchamber and examined the clothes in the wardrobe and press, after lighting an oil-lamp. She shrewdly resisted the temptation to take one of the grand opera gowns or dinner gowns, finally selecting a pretty muslin and a pelisse, gloves, and a dainty straw hat embellished with flowers. She reflected it was just as well that it was an age in which even dowagers dressed as young girls in frilly white muslin. She hoped God would not punish her, although she was not really doing anything very wrong, or so she persuaded herself. The fact that she was able to return to her room unobserved and hide the clothes in her wickerwork basket under the bed eased her conscience further. If she had been doing something wicked, God would have made sure that she was found out.

*　　*　　*

Captain Manners called on his mother on the afternoon of the ball, presenting himself in her drawing-room with increasing reluctance. To his surprise, Lady Manners rose to her feet at his entrance, as did Mrs. Devenham and, looking strangely coy, they told him that they had decided to let him have a few minutes alone with Belinda. Belinda coloured slightly and smiled, a little curved smile, and looked down at her hands.

'Will you not sit down?' asked the captain when they were alone.

But Belinda only continued to smile and stand in front of the fireplace.

'Did you wish to speak to me on some matter?' he asked.

'I only say this,' declared Belinda in well-modulated tones, 'for your own good—for Lady Manners's good.'

There was a long silence while the captain waited and Belinda placed one white hand carefully on a console table and briefly admired it.

The captain had a sudden impulse to shout,

109

'Oh, get on with it!'

'You are, I believe,' said Belinda finally, 'residing at the Poor Relation Hotel.'

'Yes. But surely I told you that.'

She looked at him directly with large brown, rather protruding eyes. 'I do not approve. You should be living here.'

'The purpose of my living in a hotel,' he said evenly, 'is that I may entertain my army friends and not disturb my mother. I have already explained that.'

'You do not seem to think highly of your friends, and as they will be my friends, too, I think it is time you entertained here. Mr. Warren, for example, is a most delightful and charming man.'

'They are not all like Jack Warren. Besides, if I may remind you, you are the one who wishes to dine at the Poor Relation.'

'True. But once you arrange that, I see no reason why you do not live in your own home. I have been brought up to know that owning wealth does not mean one should squander it, and the Poor Relation is very expensive.'

'Lady, how or where or why I spend my money is my affair and always will be.'

She compressed her lips into a thin line. 'I think you owe me an apology for that remark,' she said in a governessy voice which grated on his nerves.

He realized with a shock that this petty argument could go on and on, rather like the arguments he had overheard between officers and their wives.

He suddenly smiled. 'We will compromise,' he said. 'I shall invite several of my army friends here for one of my mama's afternoons and you shall judge for yourself.'

She smiled back triumphantly. She was sure her beauty would charm even the most savage military man. Just look at the effect she had on Mr. Warren! Their mothers came back into the room at that moment, Lady Manners looking relieved that her son appeared to be in such a good humour. She had tried to counsel Belinda against telling the captain what to do or what not to do before they were even married. In fact, Lady Manners was beginning to have niggling doubts about the engagement. She herself had had a marriage arranged for her. Love had not entered into it, but then love never did. One found *that* outside marriage, provided one observed the eleventh commandment: Thou Shalt Not Get Found Out. She was beginning to suspect her son had a sentimental streak and wondered if he had caught it from low company, the way one catches an infection.

The ladies began to talk and the captain decided to invite the crudest and worst of his acquaintance to tea with Belinda. But the trouble, he mused, is that the crudest and the worst would nonetheless behave themselves over the tea-table in a lady's drawing-room.

His thoughts drifted to the owners of the Poor Relation. He was sure they would think of something.

You are being childish, mocked a voice in his head. If you are going to spend the rest of your life with this lady, why make elaborate plans to shock her so as to have some freedom away from her?

* * *

'There is a princess in our kitchens, slaving away,' said the Duchess of Darver to the duke.

'Thought you never went down there,' grumbled the duke, handing another ruined cravat to his valet. He cursed Beau Brummell for ever having made starch and intricately tied cravats fashionable.

'Lucy, my maid, told me about this gel. She is working with those two chefs from the Poor Relation as a helper. Prettiest thing you've ever seen. Went down to look at her. Such delicacy! Such an air!'

'Probably a relative of old Lady Fortescue.'

'Can't be. Even if Lady Fortescue has decided to dabble in trade, she isn't *stupid*. Why ruin the chances of a fairy-like creature like that, who could have her pick at the Season?'

'Hard to know what to do with the by-blows,' mumbled the duke, who had fathered several bastards in his time. 'But wouldn't make one a kitchen maid. Lady's-maid or something like that.'

'Exactly. There's a mystery there. You will see her this evening. She will be handing out negus for the ladies.'

The duke finally arranged his cravat to his satisfaction by pleating the starched material with his fingers. 'What looks dazzling in the kitchens,' he said with the voice of one speaking from experience, 'can look pretty tawdry when set against the members of the ton. Why, I remember...'

'Oh, spare me,' snapped the duchess. She stood up and peered in the glass. She was still a handsome woman, she reflected, provided she used enough white lead to cover the ravages of age. But certainly one of the greatest marks of age for a lady was when she was no longer courted by the gentlemen of society and had to look for lovers among the footmen.

She gave a little sigh and, like Miss Tonks, wished briefly that she could look like Frederica for just one evening.

*   *   *

Frederica stood nervously behind a table which held a bowl of negus being kept warm by a spirit-lamp, and a forest of glasses. The duke had come up and said a few words to her but had leered at her in such a way as to make her tug nervously at the low neckline of her gown

113

once he had gone.

She was also beginning to worry that some of the men who had ridden with her on the hunting field might arrive. Certainly they had only seen her dressed as a boy, with her hair hidden by a hat. She had been kept indoors from the day her father had decided to turn her into a fashionable young lady. Still, it was an unnerving thought. Also, she would be facing the very cream of society, with all their strange taboos and shibboleths, which were not applied so rigorously in the countryside.

They came in at first by ones and twos and then in crowds. There were women with feathered head-dresses and tiaras and men carrying their bicorns under their arms. The one thing they all had in common was a hard assessing stare. Everyone stared at everyone else, quite boldly, through quizzing-glasses and lorgnettes. Most of all, the men stared at Frederica, until she began to feel vulnerable, exposed, almost naked. And then, towering above the rest, she saw the handsome head of Captain Manners and the rest of the room became a blur, with only the captain's profile in sharp focus. He turned and said something to the lady on his arm and they began to approach Frederica. Her hand holding the silver ladle over the negus bowl began to tremble. Miss Tonks, who was dispensing claret, looked across and quickly summoned a footman to take her place.

Frederica brought Belinda into focus and her heart sank. She was not aware of her good looks, feeling that her father had prized her attractions too high, and only saw that Belinda was fashionably beautiful with reddish-brown hair, brown eyes, a small straight nose, and a small mouth. That tinge of red was only a little comfort.

'Good evening, Miss Frederica,' said the captain. 'May I present Miss Belinda Devenham? Miss Belinda, Miss Frederica ... Black.'

Belinda stared haughtily at the glowing vision of loveliness that was Frederica. Frederica's hand was outstretched. Belinda gave a brief nod and then said, 'Oh, good, there is Mr. Warren. Pray excuse me.'

Behind her, her mother and Lady Manners raked Frederica up and down with hard glances.

'I must apologize for my fiancée's rudeness,' said the captain.

'On the contrary, Miss Devenham was behaving just as she ought,' said Frederica. 'One does not introduce a servant to a member of the ton.'

'Frederica,' said Miss Tonks breathlessly. 'Sir Philip is in need of assistance. Jack here will serve the negus.'

Frederica curtsied to the captain and followed Miss Tonks to where Sir Philip was standing. The captain went after them, almost

115

feeling his mother's eyes boring into his back. He knew he was behaving badly, that he should immediately swing round and go and join his party, but he seemed to be drawn after Frederica as if on wires. He stood a little away, affecting to look about him, but he distinctly heard Sir Philip say, 'You are attracting too much attention, miss. Lady Fortescue suggests that you return to the hotel. If you stay, you may be subject to coarse pleasantries from the men, which is something we should have considered. Mr. Davy will escort you and then come straight back

The captain waited, seemingly unable to move until Mr. Davy was summoned, until he saw the last glimpse of Frederica's bright hair under the little tiara moving out of the room and being lost to view.

Then he returned to the recriminations of his mother, his fiancée, and Mr. Warren, who could not *believe* that he had forgot himself so much as to introduce Belinda to a *servant*.

'They are all aristocrats.'

'They are all in *trade*,' snapped Lady Manners. 'And as for aristocrats, that one who left with your servant girl is none other, I have just learned, than that actor, Jason Davy.'

'Well ... let us talk of something else,' said the captain wearily. They moved into the ballroom. He danced with Belinda, he danced with several plain young ladies who would otherwise have been wallflowers, and all the time he felt an increasing excitement rising within him. Frederica would be alone at the hotel ... alone, that is, apart from some of the guests who had not been invited and temporary staff. Belinda, he noticed, also danced two dances with Jack Warren. How well they got on together, he thought. Suddenly he could not take any more of it: the offered snuff-boxes; the languid, scurrilous gossip; the combined smells of scent to cover unwashed bodies and musk-pills to disguise the smell of rotting teeth; the posturing and bowing and primping. He approached his mother and said that an old war wound in his back was causing him considerable pain and he must leave.

'What war wound?' she asked suspiciously.

'I told you. The one from a sabre cut on my back.'

'You never told me about any war wound!'

'I did not want to worry you at the time, Mama. It only hurts occasionally.'

Jack Warren came up with Belinda on his arm at that moment.

'Here's a coil,' said Lady Manners, torn between worry and exasperation. 'Peter tells me that he is in pain from an old war wound.'

'What—?' began Jack and stopped abruptly as the captain stepped on his foot.

'Oh, dear,' said Belinda pettishly. 'We are about to go in for supper.'

'I would be charmed, honoured, to escort

117

you,' said Mr. Warren.

'Oh, good,' said Lady Manners, fixing her son with a suspicious look. 'We will talk about this further tomorrow, Peter.'

Captain Manners made his way to the duchess and presented his apologies and then escaped into the London night.

He felt he was behaving madly, badly. Frederica was probably asleep by now. To picture her sitting waiting and available in that sitting-room at the top of the hotel was folly.

As he walked along Bond Street, he ran into a party of army friends and answered their jokes and sallies, while all the time his brain screamed with impatience, longing to get away.

At last he was free. The church clocks began to strike midnight. Midnight! Surely she would not still be awake. Only the fashionables stayed up till dawn.

The hotel entrance was quiet, with only a footman and a page dozing on a bench outside the office. He made his way up the stairs to the sitting-room and gently turned the handle and opened the door.

CHAPTER SEVEN

The night has a thousand eyes,
And the day but one;

118

Yet the light of the bright world dies,
With the dying sun.

The mind has a thousand eyes,
And the heart but one;
Yet the light of a whole life dies,
When love is done.
                    —Francis William Bourdillon

Frederica had gone to the hotel sitting-room in all her finery, reluctant to take it off. She felt lost and sad. Not only did she not belong in society, she could not even attend functions. She felt miserable, thinking that there must be something blowzy about her appearance that she had to be protected from insult. She had to admit that she had nourished hopes that the captain might fall in love with her, just like in a romance, and would sweep her up in his arms, that they would be married and live happily ever after.

One look at Belinda had been enough to show her how ridiculous such thoughts were. She rose and stirred up the fire and threw on a shovelful of coal. Perhaps the best thing would be to go next door to bed and sleep and perhaps life would look brighter in the morning. She seemed to have been in the sitting-room for hours, but the little French clock on the mantel was chiming out midnight, not five in the morning, which was what it felt like. She walked restlessly over to the piano and rippled one hand inexpertly over the keys.

Then she heard the door behind her open and swung round.

Captain Peter Manners and Frederica stared at each other.

Frederica was the first to collect her wits. 'May I be of assistance, sir?'

'No ... no,' he said. He entered the room. 'I had to leave early. I was feeling unwell.'

'I am so sorry. I trust it was nothing to do with our cooking.'

'No, I left before supper. An old war wound.'

'Are you in pain? Can I fetch you something?'

'I thank you, but the pain has abated. It was a sabre cut in my back.'

'How dreadful. But you must be hungry. I, too, have not eaten anything. Unfortunately Betty and John, our personal servants, will have retired for the night. If you care to wait here, I will bring us something from the kitchens...'

'We will go together,' he said, suddenly ridiculously light-hearted.

It was only when they reached the kitchens that Frederica realized she was still wearing her tiara and jewelry. She took down a large white apron from a cupboard in the corner and tied it on. 'Pray be seated,' she said firmly, 'and I will find something. There is some cold ham and veal pie. The cellars are locked, so you will need to be content with servants' ale. If you would be so good as to draw two tankards from the firkin over there.' She moved about efficiently and deftly, putting out plates, knives, and forks, taking some little pride in showing off how easily she knew her way around.

She tossed salad in a bowl, saying quickly and nervously, 'It is such a pity you missed Despard's cooking. He has excelled himself this evening, I am sure of that,' and all the while he watched her bright figure, the light from the candles causing the pearls in her tiara to shine with a soft gleam.

'There,' she said at last. 'We are ready.' She sat down opposite him at the kitchen table.

'When you do not know what to say to a gentleman,' echoed the voice of her governess in her head, 'then ask him about himself. It is the favourite subject of all gentlemen.'

'Are you on leave for very long?' she asked.

'Until I am recalled. I had one brief leave last year, and before that nothing since I joined the army.'

'What age were you when you enlisted?'

'Sixteen. Quite battle-hardened by now.'

'I always think our soldiers look so very grand in their uniforms.'

'You would not have thought so had you seen us in the Peninsula,' he said wryly. 'I used to dream of a proper pair of boots. Can no one make boots for the British army? The trouble is that boots are so fashionable, they are still made for dilettantes rather than officers. Do you know that Sir John Shelley went to his bootmaker's in Saint James's and complained that the new pair of boots he had recently purchased had split in several places when he had first worn them? "What were you doing?" asked the bootmaker. "Why, walking to my stables," said Sir John. "Walking to your stables!" exclaimed the bootmaker. "I made those boots for riding, not walking." After the Battle of Salamanca, the Guards had walked their footwear off, so we all adopted the mode of footwear used by the Spanish muleteers. The raw hides of freshly killed bullocks were placed flat and the man's foot placed on it. A sufficient piece of hide was cut to cover the foot and a sandal was made. They proved to be so comfortable that the Guards refused to wear captured French army boots.'

'But the great Duke of Wellington is considered something of a dandy,' said Frederica. 'Would he not make an effort to see his men well-clothed?'

'Wellington said he cared little what his men looked like provided they came into battle "well appointed and with sixty rounds of ammunition." He said he never looked to see whether their trousers were black, grey, or white. He himself hardly ever wears his full uniform, preferring civilian garb of blue coat and buff breeches.'

'It must be a hard and dreary life.'

'It is not all battles. We have our balls and parties. But some officers ruin themselves by trying to maintain a luxurious life-style. A chap called Dawson was always seen surrounded by muleteers with whom he was negotiating to provide transport for his immense personal supply of hampers full of wine, liqueurs, hams, potted meats, and other delicacies brought out from England. He also had his own cooks, said to be the best in the army, as well as a host of servants from Spain, Italy, and Portugal, and even France. He was very open-handed and much loved by his fellow officers, but his stay in the Peninsula was cut short after a year. He had only a younger brother's fortune, and his debts became so considerable that he was obliged to quit the Guards.'

The captain's voice grew dreamy with recollection. 'I remember a ball we gave at Pueblo to entertain the Spanish. The officers of Don Julian Sanchez's corps had given a ball for us, so we were returning the hospitality. We constructed a huge hut and the floor was grass. For supper, we pooled our rations and punch was made in the camp kettles. The ball began at seven but at midnight we were told we were to march at dawn, which we knew would give us all about two hours' sleep. Still, the Spanish ladies and gentlemen were much pleased with the ball. Forgive me,' he added quickly. 'I must be boring you.'

'Not in the slightest,' said Frederica truthfully. 'Tell me more.'

And so he talked on, reliving old battles while an entranced Frederica listened to his pleasant voice and looked at his handsome face and wanted the night to last forever.

At last, when a pale dawn began to filter in through the grimy window above their heads and the candles started to gutter in their sockets, he rose almost guiltily to his feet.

'I have kept you up all night,' he said ruefully. 'I have talked too much.'

'I enjoyed it,' said Frederica. 'I do not think anyone has ever talked to me before. I mean apart from polite conversation. Miss Tonks talks to me, but it is not the same.'

She walked with him to the kitchen door and unbolted it. 'You had best leave this way,' she said. 'The others will be returning soon, and if they knew you have been with me, I should get a terrible lecture.'

'We have behaved most unconventionally.' He raised her hand to his lips. 'Is Mr. Davy really an actor?'

'Yes, he is. He is working with us at the moment. Why do you ask?'

'It gave me an idea, that is all. He supervises the coffee room, does he not?'

'Yes, and very successful he has turned out to be.' She giggled. 'Sir Philip is quite furious. He is jealous of Mr. Davy.'

They stood together at the bottom of the

124

area steps. A passing watchman peered down curiously at the pair in their evening dress, lit by the red light of dawn.

'May I see you again?' he asked.

All the glory of the night tumbled about her ears. She looked up at him in dismay. 'That would not be ... fitting.'

The shadow in her eyes was mirrored in his own. 'I suppose not,' he said sadly.

He went up the area steps, hearing the kitchen door being shut and locked behind him. He stood outside the hotel, irresolute, and then began to walk away from it down through the Bond Street Straits, Old Bond Street and so to Piccadilly, his thoughts in a turmoil. Had Frederica proved stupid, he thought, then it would have been so easy to forget her. But she had listened so intelligently. She had not flirted with him or said, as his fiancée and the other females of his acquaintance would have said, 'Oh, you must not horrify us with stories of war.'

He walked by the reservoir in the Green Park and heard the noises of London all about him as the rich went to bed and the poor came awake. The red of the dawn had faded, to be replaced by grey. A thin drizzle was beginning to fall and moorfowl called plaintively from the pond outside Buckingham House.

He stared moodily down at the water. He wondered for the first time what Belinda thought of him, or indeed, if she thought anything at all about him. He felt that in her eyes he was a property, like a house, to be changed and decorated and made more to her taste. And yet this was the woman he was supposed to tumble in his arms on the marriage bed. And how unexciting that would be. She would lie there like a plank, suffering what she would no doubt privately damn as his 'necessary ministrations,' which was how he had once heard a colonel's wife describing the act of love. But by the laws of society, he could not break the engagement. She must be the one to do it. Tired as he was, he decided that the first thing he should do was to find that actor and enlist his aid.

*   *   *

Mr. Davy was in the coffee room that afternoon, glad that for once the place was tolerably quiet. He marvelled at the stamina of his older colleagues who, after only a few hours' sleep, had risen to go about the hotel business just as if they had not been working all night. He himself felt weary. He usually coped very well with the business of the coffee room because he acted his part. As long as he was acting, he felt comfortable with the world.

He looked up as Captain Manners came in, reflecting it was a pity he was not an actor, because such incredibly good looks would surely have made him a success. 'Coffee, sir?'

he asked, sweeping forward and at the same time signalling a waiter to come forward.

'Yes, coffee,' said the captain. 'I am weary.' He sank down at a table near the window. 'Will you join me, Mr. Davy? I have a proposition to put to you.'

Mr. Davy ordered coffee for himself and gratefully sat down. Like most men of the Regency, he wore shoes a size too small for him and his toes were pinched.

The captain waited in silence until the coffee had been served and then said, 'I would pay you handsomely for the acting abilities of some of your friends and of yourself.'

'How many?'

'Four. Yourself and three others.'

'Are we to put on a play for you or your family?'

'No, what I want is this. I enjoy my freedom here and I told my mother, Lady Manners, that the reason I stay in a hotel and not at our town house is because I wish to have a place to entertain my army friends, they being, or so I said, too uncouth for a lady's drawing-room. I wish you and some acting acquaintances to masquerade as friends of mine. You are to be loutish and uncouth.'

'We will need to have genuine military uniforms,' said Mr. Davy, looking not at all taken aback by this odd request because he privately thought the whole of society to be slightly touched in their upper works.

'Have you ever seen any army officer wear his uniform when off duty?' demanded the captain. 'Civilian clothes will do.'

'Thanks to Colonel Sandhurst's generosity,' said Mr. Davy, 'I can make myself presentable. But there will be a difficulty in making my friends elegant enough.'

'I do not want them elegant,' said the captain with a tinge of exasperation in his voice. 'As I said, I want them uncouth. Go and study the Corinthians who frequent Limmer's, if you have not done so already. They must be prepared to slouch and spit and swear. I do not expect them to emulate coachmen, like some of the Corinthians, and file their teeth to points, but a few snuff-stains and winestains down an unclean cravat will serve admirably.'

'I think I know what to do,' said Mr. Davy, looking amused. 'To get down to the vulgar side of the business. How much?'

The captain named a handsome sum. 'When is this to take place?' asked Mr. Davy.

'As soon as you have engaged your friends, let me know.'

Sir Philip suddenly appeared at Mr. Davy's elbow. 'You may not have noticed, Davy,' he said waspishly, 'but there are several people in the coffee room demanding attention.'

Mr. Davy looked round mildly. 'They all seem to be well taken care of by the waiters.'

'But it is your job to supervise the waiters, not to sit drinking coffee.'

'Mr. Davy is sitting with me at my request,' said the captain sharply. 'I suggest you go about your own business, sir.'

Sir Philip gave a little ingratiating smile and retreated, but he marked down the captain as someone to get even with along with Mr. Davy.

He hovered in the hall until he saw the captain leave and then went back in again. It had been forcibly borne in upon Sir Philip that his warning to Mr. Davy that Miss Tonks was promised to *him* had had no effect. Miss Tonks had followed Mr. Davy around at the ball like a silly old dog, thought Sir Philip viciously.

He sidled up to Mr. Davy with his odd crabwise walk. 'What did Manners want?' he asked.

'A talk about things in general,' replied Mr. Davy with that pleasant unruffled air of his which never failed to get on Sir Philip's nerves.

'You really ought to make up your mind about our Miss Tonks,' said Sir Philip.

'In what way?'

'She is obviously eating her heart out over you, silly old fool that she is. The least you can do is to stop encouraging her attentions.' Both men were standing at the door to the coffee room. Neither noticed Miss Tonks lurking just outside the entrance.

'I have no intention of encouraging Miss Tonks's attentions,' said Mr. Davy, goaded at last.

Miss Tonks slipped away quietly. She felt

129

just as if she had been punched ferociously in the gut. She felt every bit as silly and old as Sir Philip had described her. She ran next door and gained the privacy of her room before the tears came.

'That,' Mr. Davy had gone on, 'does not stop me finding her a very good friend and a delightful lady of style and wisdom.' But, alas, poor Miss Tonks had not heard that and thought her little world had come to an end.

*   *   *

Belinda was prettily gratified to learn that Captain Manners had invited some of his friends to tea. She smiled her curved complacement smile and glanced briefly in the direction of Lady Manners—who was looking suspicious—with a sort of I-told-you-so expression.

The very best china was laid out and the teapoy, containing cannisters of teas, was at Lady Manners's side, for she preferred to make the tea herself and not leave such a delicate art to servants. As they waited for the arrival of her son's guests, she reflected uneasily that he could be recalled to his regiment at any time, and yet he had not fixed a date for the wedding. Not that she had not suggested several suitable dates to him, but all he would say was 'I cannot think of it at the moment. I will talk to you later.' And then he never did.

Belinda, thought Lady Manners, was looking at her best in a morning gown of fine muslin with a high collar and a yoke of old lace.

The captain crossed to the window and looked down into the street. He was regretting his prank. Belinda was obviously excited—well, *excited* was too strong an emotion to apply to his fiancée—but certainly animated above usual at the thought of proving him wrong. Such a shame to disappoint her.

He saw an open carriage draw up outside. Mr. Davy had done him proud. He could hear dimly their loud rough voices and he could see the swagger with which they walked up the steps. He retreated to the fireplace.

Soon he could hear the clatter of spurs on the stairs and then the butler announced, 'Mr. Trimington, Mr. Hadley, Mr. Jones, and Mr. Strange.'

Quickly memorizing the names, the captain effected the introductions. At first he thought Mr. Davy himself had decided not to come until he recognized the actor under the disguise of Mr. Strange. Mr. Davy had powdered his hair, padded out his cheeks, and somehow managed to get a large, unsavory-looking pimple right on the end of his nose. All were dressed in the sort of coachman style affected by the worst of the Corinthians. 'Mr. Strange' bent over Belinda's hand and gave it a smacking kiss, and then, straightening up, leered into her eyes. Finally they were all seated

131

except Mr. Trimington, who lounged on the floor at Belinda's feet and picked his teeth with a goose-quill.

Although Lady Manners was dispensing tea, she had arranged earlier that Belinda should act as hostess. She could not help wishing that Belinda would *sit down*, but Belinda considered she cut a better figure on her feet, and so every time she stood up, the men scrambled to their feet. At last even Belinda saw how ridiculous this was and sat down.

'I am delighted to meet Captain Manners's friends at last,' she fluted. She gave a merry laugh. 'Captain Manners frightened me by trying to tell me you would all be so *rough*. But I now see you are all well-behaved gentlemen.'

This frightened the actors, who did not know that the horrified Belinda was trying to make the best of a bad situation, and they decided they were not being uncouth enough and might lose their fee.

'Manners was always one for the ladies,' drawled Mr. Davy. 'Do you 'member that little señorita in Talavera, lads?'

The other actors came in on cue. 'Thought her parents were going to force you to marry her after the way you went on,' said Mr. Hadley. 'Demme, when we marched off, there she was, hanging on to your stirrup, Manners, and crying her pretty eyes out.'

'Foreign ladies are always so bold,' said

Belinda primly.

'Oh, it wasn't just the foreign ladies,' put in Mr. Hadley gleefully. 'Do you mind that major's wife at Ciudad Rodrigo? Thought you were going to be facing cold steel at dawn, Manners.'

'Enough!' said Mrs. Devenham suddenly. 'Such topics are not fit for a lady's drawing-room.'

'It's the tea,' said Mr. Davy apologetically. He scratched at the pimple on the end of his nose, then he took out a large handkerchief and spat into it. 'Never could abide the stuff.'

Belinda now had two angry spots of colour on her cheeks. 'Perhaps you would prefer *gin*?' she demanded sarcastically.

'That would be prime,' exclaimed Mr. Jones. 'Glass of gin and hot. See you've got the hot water there, ma'am, so all we need is the gin.'

In a voice shaking with suppressed rage, Lady Manners said to a hovering footman, 'Gin, James, if you please.'

There was a heavy silence until the gin bottle was brought in. It had been wrested from the housekeeper, there being no gin in the cellars.

As soon as glasses were poured, Mr. Davy jumped to his feet. 'Now, lads, let the ladies hear a regimental toast.' This they had rehearsed. They all stood solemnly and chanted, 'A pox on the French, bravo for Britain, confusion to her enemies and string 'em all high!' With that the four actors drained

133

their glasses—fine Waterford crystal glasses— and then threw them into the fireplace.

The ladies sat in shocked and horrified silence, looking at the litter of broken glass on the hearth. Lady Manners said in a thin voice after what seemed to the captain hours of silence but was only a few moments, 'I have a headache, Peter. Be so good as to see your friends to the door.'

But Mr. Davy did not leave without kissing Belinda noisily on the cheek, a familiarity she had not even yet allowed her fiancé.

'When you do your job, you do it well,' muttered the captain to Mr. Davy as he ushered them out into the street. 'I doubt if I will ever be forgiven.'

Mr. Davy looked up at him shrewdly. 'I understood that was what you wanted.'

The captain went slowly back up the stairs to the drawing-room. Three pairs of eyes glared at him as he entered.

'My apologies,' he said. 'But you would insist on meeting them.'

'I do not understand,' said Belinda petulantly. 'I do not understand *at all*. How can you consort with such ... *scum*? Mr. Warren is all that is charming. I expected the same good manners from your other friends.'

The captain felt a cold shiver running down his spine. He had forgotten to warm Jack. What if Jack should meet them at some function and say he had never heard of any of these soldiers? He was suddenly anxious to get away and track him down.

'I did warn you,' he said.

'I am disappointed in you, my son,' said Lady Manners severely. 'We meet many military gentlemen at balls and parties, as you know, and none of them has ever proved to be as ill-mannered and uncouth as such as you have chosen to be your friends.'

'They are brave men and fought well,' said Captain Manners, spurred by nagging guilt into adding more lies on to the ones he had already given them. He looked at Belinda. 'When we are married and billeted in army quarters, you will be expected to entertain them.'

That was when Mrs. Devenham had a Spasm and fainted.

*　　*　　*

The captain walked into White's and asked if Mr. Warren had been in that day and to his relief was told he was to be found in the coffee room.

His unease was intensified when Jack hailed him with a cry of 'How goes the fair Miss Devenham?'

The captain sank down in a chair opposite him. 'Miss Devenham is very angry with me.'

'How so?'

'I played a trick on her.'

135

'That does not sound at all like you, and what has a gentle and sensitive lady such as Miss Devenham done to deserve having tricks played on her?'

'My mother and Miss Devenham wish me to move into the family home rather than stay at a hotel.'

'A perfectly reasonable wish,' said Jack.

'I told them I preferred to stay at the Poor Relation to entertain my army friends, for they were a trifle ... er ... uncouth.'

'Oh, thank you very much. Am I included in this catalogue of uncouth friends?'

'No, no, I assure you. The ladies think you the pink of perfection.'

'So what army friends do you have that are uncouth and unfit for a lady's drawing-room? Besides, they are such high sticklers at that Poor Relation that anyone behaving with anything other than the strictest propriety would be shown the door.'

'This is difficult to explain, Jack, but I crave my freedom, and living with three ladies one of whom is my mother and the other two my fiancée and *her* mother seems to be ... to be ... a trifle ... suffocating. To that end, I hired actors to pretend to be officers and behave badly.'

'If I were as fortunate as to have secured the hand in marriage of a dazzler like Belinda Devenham,' said Jack roundly, 'then I should count myself the most fortunate of men.'

'Humour me in this,' begged the captain, 'and do not betray me.'

'Of course. But I do not understand your behaviour or approve of it. This does not have anything to do with the pretty servant at the Poor Relation?'

'What servant?'

'I gather she is the beauty who was serving negus at the duchess's party.'

'Miss Frederica is a friend of the owners.'

'That, nonetheless, puts her beyond the social pale. I trust you are not about to make a fool of yourself in that direction. It is all very well to set up an affair after you are married, but to neglect your betrothed and play pranks on her is a sad business.'

The captain's eyes were hard.

'My business, dear fellow. My business is *my* business.'

Jack changed the subject and they chatted about mutual friends. But all the while Jack's thoughts kept returning to Belinda. He was bewildered at his friend's mad behaviour. To him, Belinda Devenham was the epitome of English femininity. He liked her stately manners, and her conversation was just as it ought to be. Like most of his peers, Jack despised ladies who said anything that could be construed as either intelligent or original. As he surveyed the captain's handsome features, he almost felt the beginnings of twinges of dislike. What man of breeding could even look at a servant with such as Belinda Devenham on the scene?

CHAPTER EIGHT

To Diddle. To cheat. To defraud. The cull diddled me out of my dearee; the fellow robbed me of my sweetheart.
—*Dictionary of the Vulgar Tongue*
Captain Grose

Sir Philip went about his duties with an amiable smile on his old face, but all the while he was plotting revenge. Captain Manners was now included in these plans for revenge, for had not Captain Manners had the bad taste to befriend Mr. Davy?

And so when the captain, who was feeling obscurely guilty about the trick he had played on Belinda, not to mention his own mother, approached him to reserve a table in the dining-room for that very evening for a party, he clicked his false teeth in a bigger and more ingratiating smile than usual and said with a question in his voice, 'We shall be honoured to entertain your friends.'

'The party will consist of Lady Manners, my mother, and my betrothed, Miss Devenham, and her mother, and my friend, Mr. Warren, so that will be five of us.'

'Very good, sir.' Sir Philip bowed low and the captain looked suspiciously at the top of the old man's nut-brown wig. It was not like Sir Philip to be so oily.

Sir Philip retreated to the office to plot and plan. He bit his thumb and stared into space. There was no denying that the captain was spoony over Frederica. Sir Philip wondered what this Miss Devenham would think if she knew about that. Causing the captain embarrassment would get to Mr. Davy's ears and upset him and that at least would be a start in Sir Philip's campaign of revenge. Now if Frederica could wait table in the dining-room, that would distress the captain, and with any luck his infatuation for the girl might appear obvious to his mother and Miss Devenham. But Colonel Sandhurst and Lady Fortescue waited table and they would never allow such a thing. How was he to get rid of them for one evening?

Nothing short of an invitation from the Prince Regent would dislodge them from the hotel. Also, it might punish Lady Fortescue a little for having forgiven Mr. Davy's lies. Although, thought Sir Philip sourly, she had been proved right. The gossip about her being Prinny's latest had died very quickly.

Why not get the colonel and Lady Fortescue an invitation from the prince to Clarence House? They might find it odd to get such a last-minute invitation, but the honour of it all would wipe any doubts from their minds. Sir Philip picked up his hat, gloves, and stick and sauntered out. In the days of his poverty, he had come to know the criminal fraternity of London. He took a hack down to the edge of that notorious slum, Seven Dials, and went up the unsavoury, rickety steps of a tenement to the home of a forger, Johnny Connors.

He rapped on the door, which was eventually opened a crack and a rheumy eye glared out at him. 'Long time since we met, Johnny,' said Sir Philip cheerfully.

'Welcome, your lordship,' cried the forger, opening the door wide and elevating Sir Philip to the ranks of the peerage. 'We ain't done business this age, and don't you look a downy cull.' He fingered Sir Philip's lapel. 'Prime stuff there.'

'Weston's best superfine,' said Sir Philip airily. 'Did you hear I'm a hotel owner?'

The forger shuffled over to a table and jerked out two chairs. 'Everyone's heard that,' he said. Johnny Connors, Sir Philip realized with a pang, was looking singularly old and decrepit. Everyone he had ever known was slowly falling to bits with the passing years.

'So what's your pleasure?' asked Johnny.

Sir Philip explained about the invitation.

The forger sucked at his broken teeth. 'It'll cost you. Normal invitation, even from Lady Silly or somebody, ain't much, but forging invitations from the prince is dangerous.'

'The couple it's meant for won't get to the authorities,' said Sir Philip. 'It's for Lady Fortescue and Colonel Sandhurst, my partners, and they won't go to the Runners. Need it now.'

'Got to have the royal crest on it. That takes time.'

Sir Philip smiled. 'If you ain't got a block in your print-shop with the royal crest on it, then I'm an idiot. You've been forging army papers and tax papers and customs papers for years.'

'Got King George, long may he reign,' said the forger cautiously. 'Prince of Wales is different.'

Sir Philip took a couple of gold sovereigns out of his pocket and began to toss them idly up and down. 'Bet you've got that as well,' he said.

Johnny seemed hypnotized by the gold. He suddenly grinned and stood up. 'We'll go to the shop,' he said.

*   *   *

'Sir Philip! Sir Philip!' Lady Fortescue's imperative voice rang out through the hotel late that afternoon.

Sir Philip scuttled out of the office. 'This has just arrived,' said Lady Fortescue, holding out a crested invitation. 'The colonel and I have been invited to Clarence House. This evening!'

'Why have they not thought to invite me?'

141

demanded Sir Philip with well-manufactured rage.

'I neither know nor care,' snapped Lady Fortescue. 'This is a royal summons, a very great honour. You will need to cope with the dining-room yourself tonight.'

Sir Philip took the invitation from her. 'How did this arrive?' he demanded suspiciously, thinking at the same time that he was surely a better actor than Mr. Davy.

'That is what is so odd. It was Jack found it at the bottom of the post-bag. He says he was sure he emptied out the post-bag this morning, but it must have become lodged there. Goodness knows how long it has been there. We sent Jack along to Clarence House with our acceptance.'

Sir Philip silently cursed. It was he who had told Jack to check the post-bag after having put the forged invitation in it. He should have realized that of course Lady Fortescue would send her acceptance. He could only hope and pray that no servant from Clarence House would arrive with a message from the Comptroller of the Royal Household to say that no such invitation had been sent.

'You sure someone isn't playing a joke on you?' he sneered. 'I mean, why ask the pair of you?'

'We are obviously in favour,' said Lady Fortescue haughtily. 'I am sorry you have not been asked as well, but it is nonetheless an honour to all of us.'

'Pah!' said Sir Philip and then hugged himself with glee as Lady Fortescue took back the invitation and swept off.

Correctly assuming that Lady Fortescue and Colonel Sandhurst would be too busy getting ready for the big event to bother much about what was happening in the hotel, Sir Philip went down to the kitchens.

Frederica was there, rolling out pastry and talking in bad French to Despard, who was correcting her and teasing her. She looked so young and pretty and innocent that the very sight of her made Sir Philip pause. For the first time he wondered what Frederica would think about having to wait table on Captain Manners and his party. But then he hardened his heart. Too late to turn back now.

'My dear,' he said to Frederica. 'A word with you.'

Frederica approached him nervously. She did not like Sir Philip's pale, calculating eyes or the way he doused himself in scent.

'Lady Fortescue and Colonel Sandhurst have been invited to Clarence House this evening by the Prince Regent. A great honour. Accordingly, I wish you to dress in your best and wait table with me in the dining-room this evening.'

Frederica did not want to work in the dining-room. While she was tucked away in the kitchens, she could forget about her circumstances. But on the other hand, she could hardly refuse. So she said, 'Certainly, Sir Philip.'

'Good, good.' He rubbed his little hands.

He made his exit and left an uneasy atmosphere behind. 'What is he up to, do you think?' asked Despard.

'What do you mean?' Frederica looked surprised. 'It is my place to help out, particularly on such an evening.'

'That one always has some plot, some plan,' said the chef. 'Why did he not ask Miss Tonks or Mr. Davy?'

'As to that'—Frederica's face cleared—'he is jealous of Mr. Davy and bears a grudge against Miss Tonks because she favours Mr. Davy. I am the only one left.'

'If he is up to anything,' said Despard sourly, 'I'll take the cleaver to his head.'

*   *   *

The captain escorted his party into the Poor Relation Hotel, feeling uneasy. The only thing that reassured him was the thought that Frederica would have finished her duties for the day and would be in the apartment next door or up at the top of the hotel in the sitting-room. Every time he had dined at the hotel, Colonel Sandhurst, Sir Philip, and Lady Fortescue had been in attendance in the dining-room.

144

They were ushered to a table in the centre of the room. Lady Manners looked approvingly round at the white linen, the glittering silver, the striped wallpaper, and the heavy brocade curtains. 'Very tasteful,' she said.

Then her eyes fastened on Frederica, who was standing next to the long sideboard. 'Dear me,' she said acidly, 'there's that gel again, the one who was serving negus at the Darvers' ball.'

The captain swung round. Frederica was looking nervous and ill at ease. 'Yes,' he said coldly.

'Oh, the one you had the bad taste to try to introduce me to,' said Belinda loudly. She rapped his arm with her fan. 'You are in need of improvement, Captain Manners. I fear the army has *coarsened* your behaviour sadly. But we have been discussing your future,' she went on archly, 'and have hit on a solution.'

'That being?' asked the captain, trying with an effort not to turn around and look at Frederica again.

'Why, you must sell out,' said Belinda gaily.

The captain gave her a horrified look. 'Not too bad an idea,' said Jack Warren quickly. 'Thinking of doing the same thing myself.'

'Miss Devenham,' said the captain, who was almost glad that he had something to be angry about to take his mind off Frederica, 'I will decide my own future and choose my own friends, now or at any other time.'

145

His voice was so cold, so acid, that an awkward silence fell on his party.

*　　*　　*

Mr. Davy found Miss Tonks in the upstairs sitting-room. He paused for a moment, looking at her and wondering why her eyes were flat and guarded. 'Miss Tonks,' he said, 'I think we have a problem.'

'Which is?' asked Miss Tonks, scrabbling feverishly in her work-basket for some mending to occupy her hands and eyes.

'Sir Philip has persuaded Miss Frederica to wait in the dining-room tonight, for as you know, Colonel Sandhurst and Lady Fortescue have gone to Clarence House.'

'So Frederica told me,' said Miss Tonks. 'I did not think it a very good idea considering how the men ogled her at the duchess's, but Sir Philip said the hotel dining-room was a different matter and he would be there to protect her.'

'As I came up here,' said Mr. Davy, 'I saw Captain Manners arriving with what I take to be his fiancée along with two other ladies and a friend. They went into the dining-room. Sir Philip found me a few days ago in conversation with Captain Manners. I cannot help feeling he plans to punish the captain for having dared to speak to me. Also, it is evident from the way Captain Manners looks at our Frederica that he has perhaps formed a tendre for her. I would like to suggest we both descend immediately to the dining-room and send Miss Frederica away.'

'Gladly.' Miss Tonks got to her feet. 'Would you be surprised, Mr. Davy,' she asked as they walked together down the stairs, 'if it should prove that that invitation was a hoax?'

'Not in the slightest,' said Mr. Davy, sounding amused. 'I am sure Sir Philip is capable of going to any lengths to get revenge.'

'So you start by taking these plates of soup over to Captain Manners's table,' Sir Philip was saying just as Miss Tonks and Mr. Davy walked into the dining-room.

'Please leave, Frederica,' said Miss Tonks quietly. 'We will take over.'

'What are you about?' hissed Sir Philip. 'How dare you give orders in *my* dining-room?'

'*Our* dining-room,' muttered Miss Tonks, 'or do you wish me to make a scene? Go, Frederica.'

Dismally Sir Philip watched the bright figure of Frederica quietly leaving the dining-room. He could not protest any further, for Lord Bewley, who had not managed to secure a further outing with Mary, had decided to vent his temper and was complaining loudly that he wanted to be served, *now*.

* * *

Lady Fortescue and Colonel Sandhurst sat nervously in an ante-room at Clarence House. Their card of invitation had been coldly handed back to them. They had been told it was a forgery, but they had been commanded to wait.

'What will happen now?' asked Lady Fortescue. 'And who would play such a trick on us?'

'Sir Philip,' replied the colonel. 'Only Sir Philip could have done this.'

'Nonsense. Why?'

'He was furious that the Prince Regent came to the hotel for dinner when he was away, although how we were expected to get word to him is beyond me. Perhaps this is his nasty way of paying us back.'

'If we get out of here without being arrested,' said Lady Fortescue in a thin voice, 'I will wring that old man's scrawny neck.'

The double doors opened and an aide entered. 'Be so good as to follow me,' he said.

Stiff with age and nerves, the elderly couple rose to their feet. They were led through a bewildering succession of rooms until the double doors of an end room were finally thrown open.

'Lady Fortescue and Colonel Sandhurst, sire,' intoned the aide, thumping his tall staff on the floor.

The Prince Regent was lounging in a chair at the far end of the room. His cravat was undone and his swollen face was bloated. Lady Fortescue had the disloyal thought that he looked exactly like the cartoons of him in the print-shops.

The couple approached slowly, Lady Fortescue sinking into a deep court curtsy, proud at her age that she could still manage to perform it without falling over on the carpet.

'What's this, hey?' asked the prince. 'Forged invitation, hey?'

'Our deepest apologies, Your Royal Highness,' said Lady Fortescue, 'but we have been, it seems, the victims of a nasty trick.'

'You may be seated.' The royal hand waved. Two chairs were produced.

'We are pleased to receive you, nonetheless,' said the prince. 'Demn fine cooking at that place of yours, what?'

'You are too kind, sire,' said the colonel with a slight tremble in his voice which betrayed his nervousness. 'In the circumstances, to grant us an audience is gracious and noble and I will cherish this meeting until the end of my days.'

'Then you won't need to cherish this meeting for much longer, Sandhurst,' said the prince brutally, 'for you haven't many days left.'

Great fat sneering toad, thought the overset Lady Fortescue and then became alarmed at the sedition in her mind.

The colonel and Lady Fortescue were offered wine, which they accepted.

'It interests us,' said the prince, 'to find out

149

the reason you call your hotel such an odd name and why you stoop to be involved in trade.'

There was a little silence while Lady Fortescue and the colonel rummaged their brains for some diplomatic explanation. It was Lady Fortescue who spoke, deciding that truth would serve best.

'We *were* poor relations, sire, and hard put to it to find our next meal, relying always on the charity of our relatives. We decided to band together with members of our own kind to survive. I had the house in Bond Street, sire, and it was our partner, Sir Philip Sommerville, who suggested the idea of a hotel.'

'But why call it the Poor Relation? Why not The Grand or The Palace?'

Lady Fortescue threw him a roguish look. 'We thought our relatives would be so ashamed of us that they would come and buy us out.'

The royal eyes stared at her fixedly and Lady Fortescue wondered if she had overstepped the mark. And then the royal jowls began to shake with laughter, and about the room the friends and courtiers began to laugh as well.

'Demme, we like you,' said the prince. 'We will dine with you again. We would like some of the pastries that chef of yours does so well.'

'Sire,' said the colonel, 'we shall send you a tray of them tomorrow.'

'Then you have our gracious permission to

150

put our arms above your door.'

All nasty thoughts about this prince faded from Lady Fortescue's mind, to be replaced by a wave of sheer gladness. She could see the royal arms now, under them a sign proclaiming 'By Royal Appointment to His Royal Highness, The Prince of Wales' gleaming above the hotel entrance.

The prince waved his hand to signal that the interview was at an end.

The colonel and Lady Fortescue rose and backed towards the door, the colonel bowing and Lady Fortescue curtsying as they went. In dignified silence, they followed the aide back through the chain of rooms and corridors and so out to their rented carriage and rented coachman.

'Well,' breathed Lady Fortescue, 'how wonderful that all turned out to be, but no thanks to Sir Philip Sommerville.'

'I am so happy, I could forgive him everything,' said the colonel. 'I was too hasty. Surely it is one of those Bond Street Loungers whom Mr. Davy has sent packing taking his revenge.'

'I would like to find out whether Sir Philip is the guilty party.' Lady Fortescue stared out at the new gaslight in Pall Mall. 'And I think I know a way to do it.'

'How?'

A smile curved Lady Fortescue's thin lips. 'Wait and see.'

Sir Philip was feeling more and more upset and guilty. In their private sitting-room, Miss Tonks and Mr. Davy were sitting together, Frederica was making a gown, the pattern spread out on the floor, and Captain Manners, of all wretched people, had come to join them instead of escorting his ladies home, which is what any true gentleman should do. The captain was still very angry that the women in his life should have put their heads together to decide his future. He had put them into their carriage and then turned back indoors, meaning to go to his own room, but his steps had taken him instead to the sitting-room at the top of the house.

Colonel Sandhurst was so elated about his visit to the prince that he had fogotten about his longing to sell the hotel. He wanted everyone to be happy—except Sir Philip. He looked at Frederica, who was continuing to cut out that pattern with a steady hand, and yet everything about her figure showed she was aware of the captain's presence. He saw the way the captain stood irresolute, looking down at her. I will make a match of it between them, he thought suddenly. I am responsible for bringing Frederica here, and it is up to me to see that she is happy.

'So now we are all here, we will tell you what happened,' began Lady Fortescue. She told

152

them how they had found out the invitation was a forgery and yet how the prince had received them and had told them he wanted a tray of Despard's pastries and that they could put the royal arms above the door. All the time her shrewd black eyes were fastened on Sir Philip, who found it hard put to make his face register all the gratification and gladness the announcement deserved.

'But,' she finished, 'the culprit is not going to get away with it. I still have that invitation in my reticule and tomorrow I plan to take it to the magistrate in Bow Street.'

'Some buck playing a trick,' croaked Sir Philip. 'Seems a bit excessive to go to Bow Street. They probably won't do anything about it.'

'What?' Lady Fortescue raised her thin eyebrows. 'A forged royal invitation? They will turn out the Runners and, believe me, the Runners know every forger in London, if I am not mistaken. Why, what is the matter, Sir Philip? You look most odd.'

'Must retire,' said Sir Philip desperately. 'Indigestion.'

He scuttled out of the room.

'Now I wonder what he will do?' Lady Fortescue looked highly amused.

'So, like myself and Miss Tonks, you think that Sir Philip played a trick on you,' said Mr. Davy. 'I think I know the reason for that.'

'Which is?'

Mr. Davy did not want to say that Sir Philip had wanted to upset Captain Manners as a way of getting back at *him*, so he said instead, 'Miss Frederica here was brought to us by Colonel Sandhurst.' The colonel threw him a warning look. Captain Manners was not supposed to know anything about Frederica. 'And so, to that end, he wanted Frederica to serve in the dining-room, knowing that that would upset both of you.'

'And did she?' asked Lady Fortescue.

'Miss Tonks and I were just in time. She was about to serve soup to Captain Manners and his party.' Lady Fortescue and the colonel exchanged glances.

'So what do you think Sir Philip will do?' asked the captain. Frederica had finished cutting out the pattern and was neatly rolling up the result.

'If I guess right,' said Lady Fortescue, 'he will wait until he thinks I am asleep and try to recover the invitation from my reticule.'

'Go into your bedchamber!' exclaimed the colonel wrathfully. 'Surely Sir Philip would not do that!'

'If the only alternative is dangling on a rope at Newgate, Sir Philip will do anything.'

Frederica closed the lid of her work-basket and sat on the sofa. The captain, who had been standing all this time, went and sat next to her.

I should really ask him if his intentions are honourable, worried the colonel. But he must get rid of his fiancée first.

'I did not like to see you subjected to such an indignity this evening,' said the captain in a low voice to Frederica.

'Some servants would consider waiting table a step up the social ladder from working in the kitchens,' said Frederica lightly.

'But you are not a servant,' he said fiercely. 'I am ... I am concerned for your welfare.'

'Miss Devenham should be your concern. But I thank you.'

'Do you know what I think?' The captain looked at her small hands and longed to take one of them in his own. 'I think Sir Philip is so jealous of Mr. Davy that anyone who befriends Mr. Davy is going to be subject to his wrath. He found me taking coffee with Mr. Davy. I think he asked you to work in the dining-room because he knew my party was to be present and he wished to infuriate me.'

'I do not understand,' said Frederica, deliberately obtuse.

His eyes searched hers and suddenly they were lost in each other. They sat very still, gazing intently into each other's eyes. Frederica felt strange and wonderful emotions surging through her body. Her bosom rose and fell and her lips trembled.

'Ahem!' said the colonel loudly. 'It has been an exciting evening, but I suggest we should all retire. Lady Fortescue and I have much to discuss in private.'

Miss Tonks felt small and old and lonely as she noticed the way the captain and Frederica rose together, rose as one person, how he took her hand and led her to the door. They were such a beautiful couple, thought Miss Tonks wistfully. And echoing her thoughts, Mr. Davy said, 'What a beautiful pair, and unless I am mistaken, very much in love.'

'What would *you* know of love?' Miss Tonks demanded and walked angrily from the room, brushing past the captain and Frederica in her haste.

'Our Miss Tonks is very upset,' said the captain as he and Frederica walked together down the stairs.

'Sir Philip is enough to try the good nature of a saint,' said Frederica.

'I should think he will have learned a necessary lesson by the time Lady Fortescue is finished with him.' The captain hesitated on the first landing and looked down at her. 'Do you ever worry about your parents, what they must be thinking, the distress they must be feeling?'

'Yes, often,' said Frederica. 'But I do not think either their distress or their worry will be too great. In fact, I think fury at my behaviour will keep softer feelings at bay for some time. I wrote to them, not saying I was here, but that I was well and safe and with a respectable family. I wrote again to them yesterday to assure them of my continuing well-being. I did not have a very happy time at home recently. I sometimes almost forget Lord Bewley is resident in this hotel and perhaps I have no longer anything to fear from him. But there are other Lord Bewleys in this world. I shall stay here for as long as they will put up with me. I cannot see any other future.'

'I wish ...' he began.

'Yes?' She looked up at him.

But he was engaged to be married and had no right to commit himself to anything.

'I mean I would consider it an honour if you would allow me to escort you to your apartment next door.'

'Thank you.'

They went on down the stairs together. He was no longer holding her hand. He wanted to take it in his again but did not dare.

They walked out of the hotel and then paused outside the door leading to the apartment which the hoteliers shared. A dusty wind blew down Bond Street, redolent of that London smell of patchouli, bad drains, horse manure, beer, and boiled mutton. Frederica's thin muslin gown flew about her body.

'Thank you for escorting me, sir,' she said, holding out her hand.

He hesitated, her hand in his. 'We ... we talk well together, Miss Frederica, do we not?'

'Why, yes.'

'So ... so surely it would not be too unconventional to meet in some public place for a chat?'

The common-sense side of Frederica's brain told her that this was a very unconventional idea. But then her whole life these days was unconventional. She nodded.

'Then when are you free? Do you have an afternoon or evening off?'

Frederica gave a gurgle of laughter. 'I am spoilt. They *make* work for me not to make me feel useless.' Her eyes sparkled. 'Tomorrow?'

He felt a surge of gladness. 'Where?'

'You forget. You know London. I do not.'

'I will take you up in my carriage tomorrow at two just outside the Green Park at the Piccadilly lodge.'

She smiled up at him and said, 'Until then.'

'Until then,' he echoed softly.

He bent and kissed her hand. She dropped a curtsy and then turned and vanished into the dark stairway behind.

CHAPTER NINE

So if I dream I have you, I have you.
For, all our joys are but fantastical.
—JOHN DONNE

Sir Philip sat fully dressed and awake, counting the hours and the half-hours. He was trying very hard not to panic, but the thought of that invitation going to Bow Street the following day made him sweat with fear. There was no honour among criminals, and he knew Johnny would shop him to save his own skin. But would the Runners—so his agonized thoughts ran—know of Johnny's existence?

There was only one thing to do. Wait until Lady Fortescue was asleep, creep into her room, and take that wretched invitation out of her reticule. When the watch called 'Two in the morning and a wet night,' he decided the time had come. In his stockinged feet, he crept out of his room and along the narrow sloping corridor to Lady Fortescue's bedchamber. Houses creak and shift at night, and he started guiltily at every sound.

He gently turned the doorknob, relieved to find the door was not locked. The room was in pitch-darkness. He took a stub of candle from his pocket and then retreated back to the corridor and after several attempts lit it with his tinder-box. Back in he went, holding the candle high. The curtains were drawn around the bed and there, over on the toilet-table, lay that reticule. He darted across the room, lit the candle on the toilet-table with his own, blew out his own candle, and put the stub back in his pocket. Then he drew the strings of the reticule and, with a sigh of satisfaction, pulled out that invitation.

Then, just at that moment, the bed curtains were pulled back and there was a great burst of laughter and there, sitting fully clothed on Lady Fortescue's bed, were the lady herself, the colonel, Miss Tonks, and Mr. Davy.

Sir Philip stared at them in horror. Their laughing faces swam before his eyes and then he collapsed unconscious on the floor, clutching his heart.

'He's bamming,' said the colonel. 'The old rogue cannot bear the fact that we found him out.'

But Miss Tonks was already crouching down on the floor beside Sir Philip. 'More lights,' she called. 'I think he really is ill.'

Candles were lit. Sir Philip's face was a nasty colour.

'Get him to his room and rouse Jack and send him for the physician,' said Lady Fortescue, alarmed.

Sir Philip was tenderly borne off to his bedchamber. They all retired to the apartment sitting-room. Frederica joined them, having been awakened by the commotion, and exclaimed in dismay when she heard the sad outcome of the joke played on Sir Philip. They all waited anxiously for the arrival of the doctor, talking occasionally in low voices, one of them rising from time to time to go to see if Sir Philip's condition had improved.

After what seemed an age, the doctor arrived. Then there was another agonizing wait to hear his diagnosis. At last the doctor joined them, shaking his head. 'He is an old man and has had a seizure,' he said, each word falling like a stone in the still silence of the room.

'Will he live?' asked Miss Tonks in a trembling voice.

'That I cannot say. I have bled him. His great age is against him.' Lady Fortescue felt death himself had walked into the room, for were not she and the colonel of an age with Sir Philip? She searched for the colonel's hand for comfort.

Miss Tonks was weeping quietly. Frederica put an arm about her and whispered, 'You were not to know the outcome. Sir Philip brought it upon himself by his spite.'

But Miss Tonks would not be comforted.

The following morning, despite having been awake most of the night, Frederica was on duty in the kitchens to help with the baking of cakes for the Prince Regent.

But to her disappointment the normally indulgent Despard would have none of it. Such an occasion was too great to risk involving an amateur. So, instead, Frederica was given writing-paper and told to make an inventory of the items in the kitchen, items that the perpetually nervous chef was always sure were being thieved.

Frederica moved about the kitchens making notes. What a lot of tiresome things there seemed to be: rolling-pins, baking-tins, cake hoops, earthenware pans, bowls, knives, forks, graters, coffee-mills, pestle and mortar, whisks, slotted spoons, mashers, syringes for icing or making biscuits or fritters, cabbage nets, pastry brush and jagging iron (marker), skimmer, salamander, fish-kettle, lemon-squeezer, pudding-cloths, weighing scales, spice- and pepper-mills, pattypans, mustard bullet, jugs, dredgers, sugar-cutters, baking-spittle, toasting-forks, dripping pans, lark-spits, and preserving pots.

Occasionally she would pause to watch Despard at his work. He and his assistant, Rossignole, were making the royal coat of arms. They rolled out pastry in the shape of a large shield. That was baked separately and then the different quarterings were baked and filled with coloured jams to make the design. The prince was notoriously fond of seed-cake, so that came next. The best seed-cake was supposed to be beaten for two hours. The heat in the kitchen rose higher, and by the time Frederica had completed only some of her list she realized she was hot and sticky and very tired and had left herself with very little time to prepare for her outing with Captain Manners.

Muttering an excuse, she sped off. As there was no hope of ever marrying the captain, she had somehow thought that by reporting for work that morning she would be doing some sort of penance to appease the gods, who might not look favourably on the behaviour of one seventeen-year-old girl. She washed and changed very quickly and it was only when she was scampering along in the direction of Piccadilly that she realized to her dismay that she was wearing one of her servant's print frocks under her cloak.

Lord Bewley was waiting in his carriage on Piccadilly near the lodge at the gates of the Green Park for Mary Jones. He saw that other servant girl from the hotel arriving and being taken up by that fellow Manners. He smiled to himself. At least *he* wasn't stooping to consort with a servant. He still believed Mary Jones to be Frederica, and for the first time in his life his lordship was deeply in love. Mary had been avoiding him of late because she did not want an affair. She had decided she wanted nothing less than marriage and that she was worth it.

*   *   *

'I am sorry I am wearing one of my working gowns,' Frederica was saying. 'I went to the kitchens this morning to help Despard and ended up having to make a dreary list of everything.'

'You look delightful,' said the captain with a smile that made Frederica's heart sing.

'Where are we going?' she asked.

'I thought you might like to see the Tower of London,' he said. 'It has the merit that no one fashionable goes there.' And Frederica's heart plummeted again as she realized that of course he could not be seen anywhere fashionable

163

with such as herself.

So by the time they arrived at the Tower and inspected the dusty animals in the menagerie and then leaned over a parapet and looked down at the river, there was a constraint between them. Frederica had decided sadly that it had been a mistake to come. They were making polite and stilted conversation, like strangers. The sun had gone in and the earlier rain was threatening to come back. At last she said in a little voice, 'I would like to return, if you please.'

In that moment, he felt mad with frustration. His dreams of kissing her had lately changed to dreams of having all of her, of tumbling her beneath him. He felt lost in the grip of a powerful obsession, and yet here she was beside him and he could not even take her in his arms.

She felt every inch of the journey back was pure misery. 'Pray do not get down,' she said when they were back in Piccadilly. He stopped his carriage and she leaped down nimbly and with a breathless little 'Goodbye' was off and running through the crowds.

Colonel Sandhurst had just visited Sir Philip to find out from Miss Tonks, who was sitting at his bedside, that the old man's condition was unchanged. He was walking along the corridor when he heard the sound of weeping coming from the room which Frederica shared with Miss Tonks. He pushed open the door and went in.

Frederica was lying face down on the bed, crying her eyes out.

'Now, then,' said the colonel, alarmed. He went and sat on the bed and patted her clumsily on the shoulder. 'Has that fool Despard been upsetting you?'

Frederica turned a face up to his that was blotched with tears. 'It is Captain M-Manners,' she sobbed.

'What's he been up to?'

'He took me on an expedition to the Tower because ... because no f-fashionable people go there.'

'This afternoon?'

Frederica nodded.

'I have to ask you this, m'dear. Did he molest you in any way?'

'Oh, no, anything but. But he was so withdrawn, almost angry with me.'

'You are in a difficult situation,' mourned the colonel, 'and it is all my fault.'

'No, no. You rescued me!'

I did it for the money, thought the colonel. Aloud he said, 'Dry your eyes and put on a pretty frock and go to our sitting-room in the hotel. Lady Fortescue has just had the delivery of some new novels from the bookshop. A quiet time reading will soothe you. Now you must excuse me. I have work to do.'

The colonel went round to the hotel and straight up to Captain Manners's room. The

165

captain was in his undress, wrapped in a splendid dressing-gown while his man brewed coffee on a spirit-stove.

'I would have a word with you in private, sir,' said the colonel.

'Leave us,' the captain commanded his servant.

'Now,' he said when they were alone, 'what is the reason for your call, Colonel Sandhurst?'

'Miss Frederica does not have her parents here to protect her,' said the colonel. 'May I ask what you were about, to take her to the Tower of London today without even a chaperone? Do I have to remind you that you are betrothed to Miss Devenham?'

'I behaved badly,' said the captain quietly. 'I wanted a little more of her company while I could. It was a bad mistake. But as to the conventions, the carriage was an open one and no one fashionable goes to the Tower.'

'As you pointed out to Miss Frederica, and so underlined the sad difficulty of her position.'

'Sir, I would gladly change her position to that of my wife if I were free, but I am not.'

The colonel felt a feeling of relief. 'Come, Captain,' he said in his best military tones. 'Where is your courage? Where your fighting spirit? Look on it as a military campaign. I am sure you can give Miss Devenham a disgust of you if you put your mind to it.'

The captain looked at him in surprise and then began to laugh. 'What an odd lot you are at this hotel,' he said. 'I will go about it directly.'

*   *   *

Sir Philip had, in fact, only swooned. He had been conscious the whole time the doctor had been bleeding him but had suffered it all without a murmur. He knew he had frightened his friends, Miss Tonks in particular, and he wanted them to go on being frightened for having made such a fool of him. But he was getting very hungry. Miss Tonks always seemed to be at his bedside. Did the wretched woman never need to go to the privy?

By the middle of the day, he felt the farce had gone on long enough. He opened his eyes a little and peered through the slits. Yes, there was Miss Tonks, her eyes red with weeping.

'Letitia,' he said in a faint whisper.

'Philip!' Miss Tonks burst into tears. 'We th-thought w-we h-had killed you.'

'I may not last much longer,' he said in a dry whisper. 'You must promise me something.'

'Anything,' said the distressed Miss Tonks, wiping her eyes.

'You must promise me that if we sell the hotel, you will come and share my declining years.'

'Oh, Philip.'

He produced what he hoped sounded like a death rattle and clutched her hand hard.

'Promise,' he urged.

'Oh, I promise,' said Miss Tonks, quite overset. 'Only don't die.'

'Thank you. I have another last request.'

'Yes, dear.'

'I am a condemned man and would like one decent meal of Despard's before I part this life.'

'I—I will go directly.' And Miss Tonks fled to spread the news that Sir Philip had come to his senses but did not have long to live.

Soon they all came into his bedroom as he was tucking into one of Despard's meat pies, gravy running down his chin.

'You look remarkably well,' said Lady Fortescue suspiciously.

'When dear Letitia here promised to be a companion to me in my declining years when we sold the hotel,' said Sir Philip, 'I felt my spirits rally.'

Mr. Davy looked curiously at Miss Tonks, who lowered her eyes and stared at the floor.

'And one thing I know,' went on Sir Philip, 'is that when Miss Tonks gives her promise, she will never go back on it.'

He tricked that promise out of her, thought Mr. Davy with a spasm of rage.

'I am sorry you had a seizure,' said Lady Fortescue, 'but it was all your own fault. You had no right to try to trick us with a forged invitation.'

Sir Philip, having finished the meat pie, handed the tray to the servant, Betty, and then lay back against the pillows and closed his eyes. 'What invitation?' he said weakly. For when he had come to his senses when they were carrying him to his room, he had felt the pasteboard of that card clutched between his fingers. He had clung on to it like grim death, and when the doctor had left to tell the others of his condition, he had nipped out of bed and thrust it into the fire.

'The one you took from my reticule,' snapped Lady Fortescue.

'Please leave,' whispered Sir Philip. 'I am nigh to death.'

'Oh, leave him,' said the colonel in disgust. 'You, too, Miss Tonks.'

When they had gone, Sir Philip tugged a copy of *Sporting Life* out from under his pillow and settled back to read, a little smile on his face.

He would not have been so happy could he have heard the conversation that was taking place between Mr. Davy and Miss Tonks.

Mr. Davy drew Miss Tonks aside as they left the bed-chamber. 'Come with me to the coffee room,' he said. 'There is something I want to discuss with you.'

Miss Tonks silently allowed him to lead her next door to the hotel. She felt stunned. She did not want to think Sir Philip had tricked her.

'Now tell me what happened,' said Mr. Davy when they were seated at a table and a waiter had poured coffee. So Miss Tonks recounted the affecting scene between herself and Sir Philip.

'The main question,' said Mr. Davy when he had heard her out, 'is whether you wish to be tied to Sir Philip.'

She gave a little sigh and then said, 'No. But I have given my word.'

'A promise that has been tricked out of you is not binding,' he said.

'He could not have done that,' cried Miss Tonks, 'Why should he?'

'Because he regards me as his rival.'

'That is ridiculous. You have no interest in me whatsoever,' said Miss Tonks bitterly.

'Miss Tonks, I owe you a great deal. I think you are a lady of great courage. I value your friendship. Sir Philip knows that.'

'Mr. Davy, I unfortunately overheard you talking to Sir Philip. You said you had no intention of encouraging my attentions.'

He flushed slightly. 'You should know that things partly overheard can be dangerous and misleading. I wished to put an end to Sir Philip's rude remarks, that is all. What do you plan to do this evening?'

'Nurse Sir Philip. In fact, I must return to his bedside.'

'Lady Fortescue's old servants can do that. In fact, I will speak to them about it myself. Go and get some sleep and we will go out together this evening, just you and me, to some comfortable but not fashionable chop-house,

170

and then we will take a stroll and look at all the things in the shops that we could buy were we extremely rich.'

Love is a great transformer. Miss Tonks raised her face to his. The blotches caused by weeping had gone and she looked at him in shy delight.

Then her face fell. 'But my promise...'

'Trust me. Sir Philip is far from dying. Take a leaf out of the old man's book. If he reminds you of it, you must be terribly sympathetic and say he said no such thing, that he was rambling and that his dire illness must have given him fantasies.'

'You mean I should *lie*.'

Mr. Davy's eyes sparkled. 'Why not?'

Miss Tonks clasped her long thin hands together. On the one side was a vision of sitting that evening beside Sir Philip's bed. On the other, she saw herself sitting in a chop-house with Mr. Davy—the blue silk, and perhaps it was not too late in the year to wear that little straw hat with the blue silk flowers—and chatting easily.

'Very well,' said Miss Tonks.

'What does that mean? To lie or not to lie?'

Miss Tonks gave a sudden, almost impish grin.

'To lie,' she said.

*　　　*　　　*

171

Sir Randolph Gray and his wife were heading for London. 'I told you Bewley was the knowing one,' he said. 'I told you it would all come about.'

For the happy couple had received a startling letter from Lord Bewley in which he said he had successfully courted Frederica— although the naughty puss was going under the name of Mary Jones and pretending to be common—and that he wished to ask for her hand in marriage.

'But do we wish to be *seen* at this Poor Relation Hotel?' ventured Lady Gray timidly. 'I was under the impression that we had not yet paid our bill. Also, Lord Bewley has said nothing about the ransom, and what was that all about?'

'Listen, Bewley will have it in hand, and if he's so keen to marry Frederica, he'll even pay our shot. He says he loves her, that he's in love for the first time. I'm surprised Frederica got him up to the mark. I used to think her as spiritless as you.'

But Lady Gray was used to her husband's insults. She lived for her work in the still-room and for the tapestries which she stitched at and had stopped paying much attention to what he said a long time ago.

When they arrived at the hotel, Sir Randolph was relieved to find there was only a footman on duty in the hall. In answer to Sir Randolph's statement that they were expected, he led the way up the stairs.

Lord Bewley greeted them with every sign of delight. He had wine and cakes sent in and then, with a broad grin and a wink at Sir Randolph, he said to the servant, 'Fetch Mary Jones here.'

For a brief moment as they waited, Lord Bewley felt a qualm of unease. Perhaps he should have proposed to the girl first.

There was a light step in the corridor and then the door was opened and Mary walked into the room.

Lord Bewley stood up and took her by the hand. 'Say good day to your parents, my chuck.'

There was a long silence. Then Lord Bewley looked at Mary goggling at Sir Randolph and his lady and saw that they were looking at her open-mouthed. His brows went down. 'What's amiss?' he barked.

'That is not Frederica,' said Sir Randolph. 'Where is my daughter?'

'Here,' said Lord Bewley, giving Mary a shove.

'That is not Frederica,' echoed Lady Randolph, her voice trembling. 'I want my daughter.'

Lord Bewley glared at Mary. 'I thought you was their daughter.'

All Mary's hopes of a noble marriage fell about her ears. In those few moments, she saw clearly why Lord Bewley had treated her with

173

such respect. But, with a certain dignity, she drew herself up and said, 'There is a girl called Frederica working here. I thought she was some relation of Lady Fortescue. I will fetch her. I have never at any time tried to mislead Lord Bewley.'

She turned and walked out of the room, her head held high. She went straight down to the kitchens.

For the first time she surveyed Frederica's beauty clearly and felt a lump rising in her throat. How could she ever have hoped to marry such as Lord Bewley? But fierce pride kept the tears at bay.

'You are to come with me,' she said to Frederica.

Frederica followed her up the stairs. She drew back when she saw that Mary had stopped outside Lord Bewley's room. 'I cannot go in there,' she exclaimed.

In a sudden fury, Mary seized her arm, opened the door and thrust Frederica inside.

Her parents rose and stared at her, at her mob-cap and apron and at the dab of flour on her nose.

'You'll get a whipping for this,' snarled Sir Randolph. 'Yes, and you'll do as you're told and marry Lord Bewley here.'

'Is that Frederica?' asked Lord Bewley gloomily. 'Don't want her.' He looked hopefully towards the doorway, but Mary had gone.

'And I am not going anywhere with you,' said Frederica to her parents. 'I am staying here.'

'You have no rights,' said her father, his temper mounting. 'Want to see the family name dragged through the courts?'

'Who was it who kidnapped you and demanded ransom for your return?' asked Lady Randolph.

'Oh, that was this lot here,' explained Lord Bewley. 'You left them with a whacking bill and they ransomed Frederica to get what you owed. I paid it, so you now owe me that as well.'

Frederica had gone paper-white. 'And Colonel Sandhurst said he was offering me refuge because he was sorry for me. I thought they were the first and only friends I ever had.'

'Didn't tell you, did they?' Lord Bewley looked at her with a certain amount of sympathy. 'True, all the same. Ask 'em.'

'I'll have the lot of them at Bow Street,' howled Sir Randolph.

'You'll look just like the silly mean man you are,' barked Lord Bewley, made bitter by rage and disappointment. 'Everyone sells their daughters in this day and age, so long as it's never openly admitted. You take this lot of hoteliers to court and you won't have a shred of reputation left ... not that you haven't much to start with anyway. Shoo, the lot of you. Sick of the lot of you.'

'I shall pack and come with you, Father,' said Frederica. 'There is nothing left for me here.'

*   *   *

Jack Warren was worried. His friend, Captain Manners, appeared well and truly drunk, and offensive with it, too.

'S'pose I musht go and call on old leech-face,' slurred the captain, getting unsteadily to his feet and stumbling on the oyster shells strewn about the coffee-house floor. He had insisted on taking Jack to this coffee-house in the Strand and had proceeded to drink brandy at a great rate.

'Who are you talking about?' demanded Jack, following him out.

The captain executed a crazy bow and then minced along the Strand. 'Who else but my dearest Belinda with her bulging eyes and thick waist.'

'How dare you insult the most beautiful creature in London,' cried Jack. 'I have a good mind to call you out.'

The captain came up to where a boy was holding the reins of his horse. He tossed him a coin as he swung himself up into the saddle. He looked down mockingly at Jack. 'You want her yourself,' he jeered. 'And you haven't got a hope.'

And then he rode off down the Strand in the

direction of Temple Bar.

He's crazy with drink, thought Jack. At least he's gone the wrong way. I must get to Miss Devenham first and warn her.

He signalled to his tiger, who brought his carriage up, and Jack climbed in and drove off as fast as he could.

Miss Belinda Devenham was 'at home' alone but graciously pleased to receive him. Her maid was present and the door of the drawing-room left open, so that the conventions were observed.

But Jack threw a nervous look at the maid and said, 'I must speak to you privately. Send your maid away, if only for a few moments.'

'That would not be correct,' said Belinda with a smug complacency which would have infuriated her fiancé had he been there to see it.

'But I am come to warn you,' he hissed.

Belinda was intrigued. She waved a hand at her maid and said, 'Leave us.'

When the woman had gone, she turned to Jack and said, 'I trust what you have to tell me warrants the unconventionality of our situation.'

'Captain Manners is very drunk and insulting and is on his way here. Do not admit him.'

'Gentlemen will drink too much,' said Belinda severely. 'But as we are to be married—'

'No, no,' gabbled Jack. 'You do not
177

understand. His insults are directed at you. And all because he is madly in love with some servant.'

'What insults? What servant?' demanded Belinda.

'He is so far gone in drink as to claim that you have a thick waist and protruding eyes,' said Jack. 'And the servant is that girl at the Poor Relation. And, worse than that ...' He took a deep breath and decided to sink the knife further into his friend's bosom. 'Those so-called army friends of his were nothing more than actors he had hired to trick you. Oh, Miss Devenham, he don't want you, but I do.' Jack sank on one knee. 'I lay my heart before you.' He bowed his head.

Belinda, although consumed with rage at the insults against her looks she had just heard, was nonetheless taken with the romantic picture Jack Warren made.

And then she thought that the best revenge she could get on the captain would be to spurn his suit.

'You may rise,' she said. 'My feelings towards you are not without warmth. You may speak to my mother and gain her permission to pay your addresses to me. When Captain Manners arrives, be he drunk or be he sober, I will tell him I want to have nothing more to do with him.'

'He comes now,' said Jack, rising and seizing her hand. There was a noisy altercation from

178

the hall as the butler tried to stop the captain from going upstairs, and then came the captain's raised voice, 'Where is my beloved cod-face?'

Belinda clutched tight hold of Jack's hand and together they faced the doorway. At the sight of the captain swaying on the threshold, she threw back her head and said, 'Begone! I can never be yours. Our engagement is at an end. My heart is given to Mr. Warren here.'

The captain debated quickly whether to hurl a few insults at her just to make sure her intention remained firm and then decided against it. Jack might call him out and Jack was a dreadful shot and a worse fencer.

So he said, 'On your own heads be it. Shend a notish to the papers in the morning.'

He then lurched off down the stairs. The butler handed him a note and said, 'This has just arrived by hand.'

The captain twisted it open. It was from Colonel Sandhurst. Frederica's parents had arrived and were taking her away, it read. The butler was to say afterwards that whatever had been in that note must have been deuced sobering, for the drunken captain immediately became a cold and determined-looking man.

CHAPTER TEN

What is love? 'tis not hereafter;
Present mirth hath present laughter;
What's to come is still unsure:
In delay there lies no plenty;
Then come kiss me, sweet and twenty,
Youth's a stuff will not endure.
—WILLIAM SHAKESPEARE

Lady Fortescue, Colonel Sandhurst, and Miss Tonks could never remember having been so guilt-stricken before. Frederica faced them all in the office and said in a quiet voice which was more terrible to their ears than if she had ranted or raged, 'It is better I go home. I have been sadly deceived. You should have told me your only interest in me was to get money from my parents.'

'My dear ...' began Lady Fortescue.

Frederica held up a hand. 'No, there is no explanation to possibly excuse your behaviour. I have left my work dresses. Perhaps the next gently bred female you trick in order to secure money will be glad of them.'

She turned on her heel and walked out.

Her parents were waiting for her in the hall, grim-faced.

'Out to the carriage,' ordered Sir Randolph.

Frederica turned and took a last look round.

180

She hated the hoteliers for having tricked her, for having pretended to like her and care for her, and yet the days she had spent here would probably, she thought sadly, be the happiest days of her life.

She was just about to climb into the carriage when Captain Manners came riding hell for leather down Bond Street. 'Stop!' he shouted at the top of his voice.

'What now?' demanded Sir Randolph. 'Don't stand there with your mouth open, girl. Get inside.'

But the captain had mounted his horse on the pavement. He leaned down from the saddle. 'I wish to have a word in private with your daughter, Sir Randolph.'

'My daughter is going home with us!' howled Sir Randolph. 'I do not know who you are, or care. Frederica, do as you are bid.'

But Frederica put her hand up to the captain and said, 'Goodbye.'

Lady Fortescue, Colonel Sandhurst, and Miss Tonks had moved out to the front of the hotel.

In front of all the watching eyes, the captain seized hold of that little hand and pulled Frederica bodily up onto the saddle in front of him and, spurring his horse, he rode straight off down the pavement of Bond Street, scattering pedestrians.

'Get the watch, get the constable!' shouted Sir Randolph.

The colonel stepped forward, a smile of relief on his face.

'That was Captain Peter Manners,' he said. 'The *rich* Captain Peter Manners, and if I am not mistaken he will shortly be returning to this hotel with your daughter safe and sound, and he will ask your permission to marry her.'

*　　*　　*

The captain slowed his hectic pace. 'Where are we going?' asked Frederica, half laughing, half crying.

'Anywhere where we can talk,' he said in her ear as he held her tightly against him.

He finally ended up in Berkeley Square. He swung down and tethered the horse to the railings and then lifted Frederica tenderly down.

He tucked her arm in his and led her onto the square of grass and sat her firmly down on a bench.

He stood looking down at her and then he smiled and took out a handkerchief, dropped it on the ground and then knelt in front of her and took her hands in his.

'Miss Frederica Gray,' he said, 'I am a free man. Miss Devenham does not wish to marry me. Will you do me the very great honour of becoming my wife?'

Frederica looked down at him, dazed, her bewildered senses trying to become used to being snatched from hell to heaven.

'Why?' she asked.

'Because I love you with all my heart.'

'My parents will not allow it.'

'I do not care. We will go to Gretna. We will be married whether they approve or not. What do you say?'

'Yes,' said Frederica. 'Oh, *yes*.'

He sat beside her on the bench and gathered her into his arms. He placed his hands on either side of her face and his mouth descended hungrily on hers. People passed and repassed across the grass, looking curiously at the entwined couple.

The Duchess of Darver, walking her pug, raised her lorgnette and studied the pair.

'Goodness,' she said to her maid, who was a pace behind her. 'That is that servant gel with Manners. Poor thing. Mark what can happen to a servant girl, Lucy.'

'Yes, Your Grace,' said Lucy meekly, but staring at the handsome captain so lost in love, she was thinking that for such an experience she would happily allow herself to be ruined.

The captain and Frederica were oblivious to the watchers as they kissed and hugged and kissed again. Rain began to fall, and about them people hurried for shelter and still they kissed, raindrops trickling round their joined mouths.

At last the captain reluctantly freed her. 'My horse must not be allowed to stand in the rain.'

Frederica laughed up at him. 'Do you mean it is all right for me to get wet but not for your horse?'

'Something like that. Now to face your parents.'

'I wish I did not have to see those hoteliers ever again,' said Frederica as she and the captain walked back across the grass.

'Why? I thought they were most kind to you?'

Frederica told him about the ransom.

'Well, that's very shocking, to be sure,' said the captain, 'but I am most indebted to them. It was Colonel Sandhurst who told me to face up to the task of disaffecting my fiancée. It was Colonel Sandhurst who sent me an urgent note to say your parents had arrived and that you were leaving. They have behaved reprehensibly but you cannot say they do not care for you.'

'But to do such a thing!'

'They are very unconventional and quite eccentric, but were they any other way we would never have met. I am afraid you are going to have to forgive them.'

*   *   *

Lady Fortescue, the colonel, and Miss Tonks were sitting with Sir Randolph and Lady Gray in the hotel coffee room, being waited on by Mr. Davy.

The angry colour had left Sir Randolph's

face. 'So you tell us, Colonel,' he said, 'that this Captain Peter Manners is the wealthy son of Lady Manners, who resides in Berkeley Square, that he is a nephew of Lord Billington, who has those vast estates in Essex?'

'Yes, indeed,' said the colonel. 'We have Frederica's best interests at heart. I made it my business to find out about him. Even if, by any chance, the widowed Lady Manners disapproves of his marriage, he is rich in his own right, having been left a healthy sum three years ago by an aunt.'

'Well, well, well.' Sir Randolph rubbed his hands. 'Why didn't he just approach me and ask leave to pay his addresses, hey?'

Lady Fortescue's voice was tired. 'Your daughter ran away from home to escape being forced into a marriage with a man she had never even met and a man considerably older than she. Captain Manners knows this.'

'Frederica was always flighty.'

Lady Gray spoke for the first time. 'She was never flighty. She was ruined by your determination to make her into a boy. And then you found out you could *sell* her at a profit. You have only yourself to blame for this mess, Sir Randolph, and if everything turns out for the best, it is more than you deserve.'

'You stupid woman!' he raged. 'How dare you blame me!'

'Goodness knows,' said Lady Gray quietly and relapsed into her usual abstracted silence.

185

                    *   *   *

Lord Bewley paced up and down his hotel
room. His fury had long burnt out, to be
replaced with a desolate feeling of loss.

He had to admit that Mary Jones had only
spoken the truth when she had claimed not to
be Frederica. He missed her enthusiasm and
laughter and her glowing good looks. He
missed the sheer pride he took in being seen out
with her. Dammit, she dressed like a lady and
of late had even begun to speak like a lady. He
thought of his dark and gloomy home in the
country, which all too recently his mind's eye
had decorated with the glowing Mary to
brighten his life.

He stared at himself in the looking-glass. His
face was still beefy and florid, but his small eyes
held the look of a lost child.

Then, in the depths of his despair, he began
to hear a nagging little voice in his head. Why
not marry her, after all? They could go
everywhere together and have laughs and
cuddles and she would be all his. Hope grew
somewhere inside him and burst into a flame.
He reached out and rang the bell and said to
the waiter who answered it, 'Fetch Mary Jones
here.'

'That will not be possible, my lord. Mary has
left.'

'Address?' barked Lord Bewley.

'I do not know, my lord.'

'I'll find it myself.' He pushed past the waiter and strode off in search of Lady Fortescue.

He ran her to earth in the coffee room in the middle of what appeared to be a champagne party, the central figure being a glowing, if wet, Frederica.

Lord Bewley scowled down at Lady Fortescue. 'A word with you,' he said.

*   *   *

Mr. Harry Jones stared in bewilderment at the rather truculent lord who was facing him across the greasy cluttered table of his tenement home. The children had been sent out to play in the street. Mary, Lord Bewley had been told, had been sent to the bakery for stale bread.

Mr. Jones found his voice. 'You want what?'

'To marry Mary.'

'Why?'

'I love her.'

'Oh,' said Mr. Jones, looking wildly around for his wife and then remembering she had gone out to her scrubbing job in the West End.

'She ain't got a dowry,' ventured Mr. Jones.

'Didn't expect one,' said Lord Bewley.

'Oh.' Mr. Jones scratched his armpits and looked at the dirty walls for help.

'So what do you say?'

'Here's our Mary,' said Mr. Jones with relief. 'Ask 'er. Ain't got nuffink to do wi' me.'

187

Mary thought she had suffered enough humiliation to last a lifetime until she walked in and saw Lord Bewley with her father.

But she had spirit enough to say, 'You should not have come here, my lord. I never pretended to be anyone else.'

'I want to marry you,' said Lord Bewley bluntly. 'Come on. Let's go.'

Mary stared at him. 'You'd best come back to my place in the country,' Lord Bewley went on. 'Got a fright of an aged aunt in residence. She'll do as a chaperone.' He looked about him. 'As for this horrible family of yours, I can't have in-laws in conditions like this. They'd best start packing and I'll find a place for them on the estate.' He glared at Mr. Jones. 'Have your stuff packed up by next week and I'll send a carriage to convey you and a fourgon for your traps. I think that handles everything.'

'She ain't said she'd marry you,' said Mr. Jones, rallying, and exhibiting a trace of his daughter's spirit.

Suddenly all truculence left Lord Bewley and he looked at Mary. 'Please say yes,' he said. 'We'll have lots of larks.'

Mary's face glowed in the dark, dingy room. She dropped a curtsy.

'Yes, my lord,' she said demurely.

* * *

That evening Sir Philip looked up hopefully as his bedroom door opened. But it was not Miss Tonks, but the poor relations' personal servants, Betty and John, who came in bearing his evening meal.

'Where's the Tonks creature?' demanded Sir Philip pettishly.

'Don't know,' said Betty, putting a tray on the bed while John built up the fire. 'All sorts of commotions going on today.'

'Such as?'

'Don't know, sir,' said Betty. 'Not my place to ask.'

Sir Philip was so used to being at the centre of things in the hotel that he thought he would die with curiosity. After the servants had left he picked at his food and then found he could not bear it any longer. He rose and doused himself in scent, changed and dressed and made his way next door to the hotel and up to the sitting-room.

Lady Fortescue and the colonel were sitting talking when Sir Philip walked in. They both looked up in surprise.

'Why, Sir Philip!' exclaimed Lady Fortescue acidly. 'Not at death's door, I see.'

'Stow it,' he said rudely. 'Where's the Tonks?'

'Gone jajuntering about the Town with Mr. Davy,' replied the colonel with a rare gleam of malice in his blue eyes.

'That's just fine, that is. She's supposed to be

189

at my sick-bed.'

'I don't think you're sick at all,' said Lady Fortescue. 'Touched in your upper works, but not sick.'

'Ho! If that's your attitude, I'm going.'

Lady Fortescue smiled at him sweetly. 'Without hearing the gossip?'

Sir Philip, who had half-risen from his seat, sat down again. 'What gossip?'

So he heard all about Frederica's engagement and then the startling news that Lord Bewley had proposed marriage to the chambermaid, Mary Jones. Lady Fortescue relished telling Sir Philip about the colonel's part in getting the captain and Frederica together and how Frederica had so prettily forgiven them all for using her to collect money.

Sir Philip scowled. He felt he was losing his grip on affairs. If it went on like this, they might even decide they could do without him.

*　　*　　*

Miss Tonks at first felt she had really come down in the world. It was such a very ordinary chop-house full of such undistinguished people. But what, she lectured herself, had hanging on to gentility brought her in the past? Despair and hunger, until Lady Fortescue and Colonel Sandhurst had come on the scene. She began to relax.

'That is a very fetching bonnet,' said Mr. Davy, and quite suddenly the chop-house changed in front of Miss Tonks's eyes and became as exotic a place as Clarence House. Mr. Davy asked her to tell him some of the adventures of the poor relations, and Miss Tonks reflected later that she had never talked so much in her life and to such an interested audience.

'Now what?' she asked gaily when they finally left the chop-house.

'Why, we go shopping,' said Mr. Davy, 'for all the things you would like in your mansion.'

'I will never have a mansion, sir.'

'That is not the way to think. What would you like?'

'Not a mansion,' said Miss Tonks slowly, 'but a comfortable residence, perhaps in the country but quite near a large town so that one would not feel too out of the world.'

He laughed. 'A thatched cottage?'

'Oh, no. Thatch means rats and things. I do not want somewhere old. A nice trim building perhaps, with a portico and two floors. Four bedrooms would be enough, and a drawing-room and dining-room and a kitchen with a modern stove, for I would not like servants who had to suffer. Not many servants. Just a cook-housekeeper, two maids, a boy, and a man to do the outdoor work.'

He stopped in front of the brightly lamp-lit windows of a china shop. 'For the dinner service?' he prompted her.

'Oh, Wedgwood, certainly. And perhaps that pretty service for tea, but I would like a silver pot because it keeps the tea much hotter.'

Laughing, they went from window to window, 'buying' furniture and materials for hangings and upholstery until they drifted arm in arm back to Bond Street.

'And books for the long winter evenings,' said Miss Tonks, stopping in front of a bookshop. 'Not bought by the yard but carefully chosen. All the books I have ever wanted to read.'

Sir Philip, on his way to Limmer's, stopped on the other side of the road and surveyed them sourly. Miss Tonks was wearing what he damned as a 'silly little bonnet.' He could hear her light laughter and reflected it was a long time since he had heard Miss Tonks laugh like that.

Davy would really have to go, thought Sir Philip, and so he went on his way to Limmer's to plot and plan while Miss Tonks and Mr. Davy, blissfully unaware that they had been seen by him, continued their window-shopping.

*　　*　　*

Five months later, Frederica and her captain were married at the little church in the village

192

near Frederica's home. It was fashionable for brides to shed tears at their wedding, particularly in the vestry when they signed the parish register, but Frederica reflected that as she had had a very unfashionable life to date and was too happy to pretend to cry, there was no need to start to follow fashion. She was still armoured in the captain's love, which was just as well as the captain's mother disapproved of her strongly, and Belinda Devenham, her mother, and Belinda's fiancé, Jack Warren, were at the wedding.

Sir Randolph was furious because Lord Bewley and his unfashionable wife were present. Not only that, but his own wife had befriended Mary, Lady Bewley, and as that friendship had strengthened, so had his wife's character and she no longer trembled in his shadow. By rights Lady Bewley should have been ostracized from the country and probably would have been had it not been for her father, who had blossomed into a land agent with a talent for making everything prosper. How this had come about no one knew for the man was barely literate, but he had conceived a violent love for the land and that land had repaid him, and so his fame had spread abroad and landowners came to study his methods and brought their wives, who were titillated at the novelty of being entertained by an ex-servant who did not behave like a servant at all.

Lord Bewley, still lost in love, had mellowed

enough to begin to enjoy rare popularity.

Jack Warren sat next to Belinda in the church and watched Captain Manners lead his bride down the aisle. They looked radiantly happy. 'I am so glad I did not make the dreadful mistake of marrying him,' whispered Belinda, and Jack tried to feel gratified but could not, for somehow she had made him sell out and the news that Peter Manners was returning to his regiment and that his bride was going with him made him depressed. He was beginning to feel almost—well, the thought was disloyal—that he had been *tricked* into proposing to Belinda.

Lady Fortescue, the colonel, Miss Tonks, Mr. Davy, and Sir Philip were all there. They were in a high state of excitement, not because of the wedding, but because a foreign prince, Prince Hugo Panič, from some principality in the wilds of Middle Europe, had commandeered most of the rooms of the hotel for the following month. News of his largesse had spread before him. He was paying a fortune to have the hotel for himself and his court. They felt their days of crime and plotting were behind them. After the prince's visit, they could finally sell up and perhaps return to society. The royal coat of arms now gleamed above the door of the hotel. They still had their standards and knew their social standing, apart from Mr. Davy, who had never had any. They also thought that dear Frederica had slightly overstepped the mark by inviting the two hotel chefs as well.

Lady Fortescue at the reception, despite her stiff views, remarked that Mary Jones was now every bit the lady she was supposed to be and not at all common. Did that not show, asked Mr. Davy, that character was worth more than breeding? But he fell silent before the amazement in Lady Fortescue's black eyes.

When the dancing began, Sir Philip secured a waltz with Miss Tonks. 'You're getting flighty,' he grumbled. 'I'm holding you to that promise.' Miss Tonks circled gracefully under his arm.'

'What promise?'

'The one you made to me on my deathbed.'

'You were rambling a lot,' said Miss Tonks seriously. 'But I do not remember any promise.'

'May God strike you dead, you old harridan,' said Sir Philip, and Miss Tonks gave him a sweet smile, noticed that the dance was over, and went in search of Mr. Davy.

*   *   *

The captain and Frederica faced each other across the bed while from downstairs came the jaunty strains of a country dance. Frederica shivered in her night-gown.

'I don't like this,' she whispered. 'I don't like this at all.'

'Come to me, my sweeting. What is it you don't like?'

'I don't like what we are about to do with everyone down there knowing what we are about to do.'

He went to the window and leaned out and closed the shutters and then drew the curtains. He walked back round the bed and felt for her in the darkness. 'Now you can't hear them.' He pulled her into his arms and began to kiss her fiercely and then he laid her down on the bed and stretched out beside her.

She shook and trembled so much that he felt a coldness steal over him. He had not envisaged making love to a frightened bride. 'What is the matter?'

'You are naked.'

He hesitated. The gentlemanly thing would be to rise and get dressed and then woo her physically by degrees in the days that followed. And then he almost heard Colonel Sandhurst's voice in his head saying, 'Take action.'

Despite her protests he reached down and eased her night-dress over her head and then pulled her naked body down the length of his and began to slowly caress her and kiss her until gradually the cold body against his began to burn and tremble, and not with fear.

At some time during the night, she said huskily, 'Liar.'

'How so?'

'No sabre wound.'

He laughed. 'The things I did and said to make you mine!'

*　　*　　*

A month later, Lady Jane Fremney was deposited with her baggage at the Poor Relation Hotel. She walked into the hall and looked about. She signalled to a footman and said, 'Be so good as to bring my bags in,' and then hoped the shabby hack in which she had arrived had driven off.

Sir Philip came out of the office and stood looking at her. He saw a tall and beautiful dark-haired woman with large sad eyes.

He went forward and bowed low.

'I am Lady Jane Fremney and I wish accommodation,' said Lady Jane grandly. 'My maid will be joining me presently.'

Sir Philip spread his little hands. 'I am afraid we have a foreign royal household in residence and they have taken up the whole hotel.'

For a brief moment, she looked lost. Then she said haughtily, 'I am tired. Have you nothing at all?'

Sir Philip thought quickly. There were the small rooms which had been used by Captain Manners, all right for a military man but hardly suitable for a lady. But he was acquisitive and so he said, 'We have a little apartment but hardly the thing for your ladyship.'

'Show it to me!'

He led the way up the stairs. Lady Jane looked about. A smile curved her lips. 'This will do,' she said.

'I will have your bags sent up,' said Sir Philip, rubbing his hands, 'and our maids will unpack—'

'No, my own maid will unpack for me.'

When Sir Philip had gone, Lady Jane removed her bonnet and threw it down. Her bags were carried in. She had no maid. Most of her cases were weighted down with stones and her heavy jewel box contained only pebbles.

A week of good food in this best of hotels was what she planned.

And then she would take her own life.

*   *   *

'All's going well,' said Lady Fortescue. 'Our royal guest is so pleased with us that he showers us with gold on all occasions. Nothing can go wrong now.'

'Pity about that French hotel over at Leicester Square,' remarked Sir Philip.

'Why, what happened?'

'A Miss Caterham committed suicide there, hanged herself in her room. Trade fell off. Her ghost is said to haunt the place. There's nothing like a suicide for ruining a good hotel. People are so superstitious.'

'Nothing can spoil *our* success,' said Lady Fortescue. 'Suicide! Our prince is too happy a man. Just imagine. A suicide here? Fiddlesticks. Could never happen!

'More tea, Colonel?'

We hope you have enjoyed this Large Print book. Other Chivers Press or G.K. Hall Large Print books are available at your library or directly from the publishers. For more information about current and forthcoming titles, please call or write, without obligation, to:

Chivers Press Limited
Windsor Bridge Road
Bath BA2 3AX
England
Tel. (01225) 335336

OR

G.K. Hall
P.O. Box 159
Thorndike, Maine 04986
USA
Tel. (800) 223–6121 (U.S. & Canada)
In Maine call collect: (207) 948–2962

All our Large Print titles are designed for easy reading, and all our books are made to last.